"I, ul birth

"I hop[...]
packag[...]r.

Unsure how to react, Irene stared at them. "What are they?"

"Open them and see. That one first." He pointed at the flat package.

She did and smiled at him. "Chocolate creams. How did you know about my sweet tooth?"

"Doesn't everybody have one? Now open the other one."

She tore off the paper and opened the box—and nearly bounced with excitement when she found an electric iron. "This makes it seem more real."

His smile widened. "That was the idea."

Irene stared at him, noting the small lines at the edges of his eyes, the firm line of his mouth. Her voice caught as she tried to speak. She tried again. "Thank you."

He opened his mouth, but closed it. Then opened it again. "The REA circus is going to be in the Springfield area soon. Would you like to go?"

She tilted her head, unable to speak, or hardly breathe. Her thoughts were so jumbled she wasn't sure she understood. "You…you want me to go with you?"

Books by Helen Gray

Love Inspired Heartsong Presents

Ozark Sweetheart
Ozark Reunion
Ozark Wedding

HELEN GRAY

grew up in a small Missouri town and married her pastor. They have three grown children. If her writing touches others in even a small way, she considers it a blessing and thanks God for the opportunity.

HELEN GRAY

Ozark Wedding

HEARTSONG
PRESENTS

If you purchased this book without a cover you should be aware
that this book is stolen property. It was reported as "unsold and
destroyed" to the publisher, and neither the author nor the
publisher has received any payment for this "stripped book."

Recycling programs
for this product may
not exist in your area.

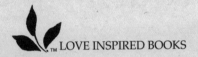 LOVE INSPIRED BOOKS

ISBN-13: 978-0-373-48725-7

OZARK WEDDING

Copyright © 2014 by Helen Gray

All rights reserved. Except for use in any review, the reproduction
or utilization of this work in whole or in part in any form by any
electronic, mechanical or other means, now known or hereinafter
invented, including xerography, photocopying and recording, or in
any information storage or retrieval system, is forbidden without
the written permission of the editorial office, Love Inspired Books,
233 Broadway, New York, NY 10279 U.S.A.

This is a work of fiction. Names, characters, places and incidents are
either the product of the author's imagination or are used fictitiously, and
any resemblance to actual persons, living or dead, business establishments,
events or locales is entirely coincidental.

This edition published by arrangement with Love Inspired Books.

® and TM are trademarks of Love Inspired Books, used under license.
Trademarks indicated with ® are registered in the United States Patent
and Trademark Office, the Canadian Intellectual Property Office and in
other countries.

www.Harlequin.com

Printed in U.S.A.

Let your light so shine before men,
that they may see your good works
and glorify your Father in heaven.
—*Matthew* 5:16

God is light, and in Him is no darkness at all.
—*1 John* 1:5

This book is dedicated to the memory of my little sister, Irene. My singing partner and best friend, she lost her life in a car accident at the age of sixteen.

Chapter 1

Missouri, 1939

Irene Delaney wrote an arithmetic problem on the blackboard and turned to face the three students seated on the bench at the front of the one-room school. "Martha, can you—?"

Bang. Pop. Bang.

A hand flew to her chest, sending the chalk sailing to the rough pine floor, where it shattered.

Children shrieked and ducked down in their desks, hands over their ears.

Another explosion rattled the door of the potbellied stove that occupied the center of the west wall. Eyes peered over desks at it.

Irene fought to control her rapid breathing. Moments later the hammering of her heart slowed as her brain figured out that one of the students had put some kind of ammunition in the stove. And there could be little, if any, doubt as to which student had done it.

The students seemed to reach the same conclusion just as Irene did. All eyes turned toward Wesley Bozeman.

"Miss Delaney," said eight-year-old Pansy Murdock.

"Yes, Pansy."

"I saw Wesley put something in the stove."

This was the last straw. Fear that had quickly turned to exasperation now became anger. Irene turned to face the lanky thirteen-year-old boy. He wore an expression of studied innocence, but it changed to defiance as her accusing stare bored into him.

"Little Miss Tattletale," he mocked, aiming a glare at Pansy. "Always making up tales."

"She may be a tattletale," another student piped up, "but she tattles the truth."

Irene drew a deep, steadying breath. "Wesley, you may stay after school to discuss this."

Lord, please give me patience. Help me guard my tongue.

Too angry to deal with the perpetual troublemaker in front of the students, she strove for calmness and continued the lesson. "Okay, Martha, can you show us how to do this problem?" She indicated the blackboard.

"Yes, ma'am." The twelve-year-old went to the board and began to write.

Wesley shot out of his seat, nearly knocking the desk over, and made for the side of the room lined with coats hanging from hooks. He snagged his and went out the door, slamming it hard behind him.

Irene did a quick assessment. Going after Wesley would mean leaving the other students unsupervised, and she doubted she could catch him anyhow. He would go home and that was fine with her. She directed her attention back to her pupils.

Irene's stomach tumbled as she peered through the windshield at the thickening snow. It was a relief when she arrived at the Bozeman farmhouse, a small single-story structure that had been painted white, and pulled her old Model T to a stop. She knew that Mrs. Bozeman had been widowed about a year ago and had four children to raise by herself, which was why Irene had delayed so long in bothering the woman about Wesley's disruptive behavior.

After school today she had offered the three younger Bozeman children a ride home if they would wait until she was ready to go. Knowing the purpose of her visit to their house, they had declined her offer and walked home as usual.

Irene pushed her hair back from her face and took several deep breaths as she walked up onto the small front porch and knocked at the door. Mrs. Bozeman was hardly a person who would eat her alive, but Irene hated conflict and dreaded the encounter. She liked teaching well enough but hated the discipline part. She wanted to find a job related to music after this school year ended. It scared her to think of leaving the familiarity of home, but she would do it to get to work full-time in a musical ministry.

Her sister, Jolene, would be ready by next fall to resume her position as teacher of the school where she had taught for the past seven years. Irene had graduated from high school and completed enough teacher training to be able to temporarily step into Jolene's shoes—as if that could truly be done—in time for her and Riley's first baby to be born. Schools had become less rigid about women continuing to teach after marriage, but the community did not want them to teach while expecting a child. But by the end of the school year Irene would be ready to move on to a job where she could use her musical ability.

When Nell Bozeman opened the door, she didn't act surprised to see Irene. A tall woman with salt-and-pepper hair, she wore a faded brown cotton dress and looked as though she might have been sick. Hands rough from hard outdoor work held a long-handled spoon. She stepped back and widened the door opening. "Come in," she said, her voice soft.

Irene brushed the snowflakes from her gray wool skirt and entered the tidy living room. She followed the woman to her kitchen, where twelve-year-old Cassie was setting the table and eleven-year-old Jenny stirred a pot at the stove. Irene didn't see ten-year-old Lonnie. Or Wesley.

"Have a seat." Nell motioned to the table and took the chair across from Irene. She glanced at the girls, then back to Irene. "Is Wes in some kind of trouble?"

Irene swallowed and then stated the blunt truth in a rush. "Someone put bullets in the stove, and they exploded. Other students say they saw Wesley do it. I asked him to stay after school, but he grabbed his coat and left."

Nell Bozeman emitted a long sigh. "He stomped into the house about two o'clock. All he would say was that Miss Delaney doesn't like him, and he wants to quit school."

Irene gasped. "That's not so. I like all my students. I just can't allow potentially harmful behavior. He has played a number of pranks that disturbed the classroom, and I've made him miss recess and copy pages from the dictionary. But today's incident was dangerous, and someone could have been hurt. I don't want to add to your burdens, but I had no choice. You need to know what's going on, and I need your help."

The woman shook her head in weary frustration. "I don't know what to do with him. He never liked school much, but since his dad died, he's been unhappy and hard to deal with."

The door opened, and the subject of their conversation entered, accompanied by Lonnie and a man in his twenties, each carrying a full milk bucket. Wesley came to an abrupt halt and glared at Irene.

Her gaze locked on the man as memory kicked in. She had seen Gavin Mathis only a couple of times since his return to Deer Lick a few months ago. With his name being different, she tended to forget that Mrs. Bozeman was his mother. No longer a scrawny, overworked boy, he was well built with broad shoulders and neatly trimmed sandy-brown hair and stood about six feet tall. Startling eyes of brilliant aquamarine, made even more dramatic by his blue shirt and black coat, beamed a heat ray at her.

He had attended the rural Deer Creek School, but he was Jolene's age. They had both finished eighth grade at the rural school and gone on to high school in town about the time Irene started school. She remembered him, but not well.

He was handsome, and he carried himself with an easy assurance that had developed in the eight or nine years he'd been gone.

Irene remembered that Gavin's dad had died when Gavin was just a small boy. His mother had remained single for several years before she married Roy Bozeman when Gavin was approaching his teens, which was why he was so much older than the four children who now attended the rural school. Gavin had left home as soon as he finished high school. The younger kids mentioned him now and then, but not often.

"Hello, Mr. Mathis," she greeted him, uneasy at that piercing glower.

"Wes says he came home early today because you pick on him. What's your problem?" His tone was biting.

Irene's hackles shot sky-high, and she sprang to her feet. "I do not pick on him, Mr. Mathis. In fact, it's the opposite. He plays pranks and constantly disrupts the class, leaving me no choice but to punish him. Which I hate," she added.

"Today's prank was not funny." Mrs. Bozeman spoke gently, directing a look of censure at Wesley. "He put live ammunition in the stove, and it blew up."

Gavin hesitated a moment. Then he put his milk bucket down and turned to Wesley. "That doesn't match what you've been telling me. What's the truth?"

Silence reigned as the boy shuffled his feet and stared down at them.

"He did it, Mom."

All eyes turned to Cassie. Standing by the table, her hands clenched at her sides, she stood firm. "Miss Delaney has to talk to him nearly every day. A lot of his tricks are funny, but what he did today scared us."

Irene could almost hear Mrs. Bozeman deflate. The woman glanced at Wesley and then at Gavin, her mouth tight.

Gavin's face turned grim. As he studied his mother's expression, Irene recognized what she thought was a silent request for approval to act. When Nell nodded, he refocused on Wesley. "I think there are some barn stalls that need mucking, and this place could use a few other cleanup jobs. I'll check when I get home from work every day to see how much you've gotten done, so you'd better come straight home from school and get to work."

Wesley's face turned red, but he didn't argue.

"Son," Mrs. Bozeman said sternly, "I expect you to behave properly in school. I don't want to hear about this kind of thing again."

Irene almost felt sorry for the boy—but not quite. She had to consider the well-being and safety of all her students. "Thank you for your support. I'll see you in the morning." She encompassed all four of her students in the farewell.

Deep in thought, Gavin vaguely comprehended the barren winter landscape as he turned off the blacktopped highway onto a rough country road. Electricity had been available in cities for years—in their own little town for over a year—but only about 10 percent of rural farms had power. Since the Rural Electric Administration was established in 1935, they'd made headway, but much work still lay ahead of them.

Skepticism abounded and created problems for the REA and the crews he managed. Fear of the unknown made farmers think twice about going into something so mysterious as power that hummed over lines and could not be seen or touched. His job as a field man was to plot a map of the homes that had been signed up and pick up as many new members as possible. Most rural people wanted electricity desperately, but the demand for it was not universal. Some worried about getting in debt to the government, and even the five dollars to sign up was not a sum to be taken lightly.

A line had to be financially worthwhile, which meant there had to be at least three hookups per mile. He needed one more hookup in that mile up ahead, and Sam Delaney was the holdout he needed.

The name resurrected his recent encounter with the

man's daughter. A dainty thing, the young teacher was a far cry from the rough-and-tumble tomboy he remembered riding up and down the road on an old bicycle day and night. Her delicate mouth, high cheekbones, black hair and glinting black eyes rimmed by long black lashes filled his mind, as they had all last night and this morning. She had a soft, natural prettiness that he liked better than if she had been flashy. He remembered the older sister, Jolene, well, but Irene had been just a kid when he left home nine years ago. She certainly wasn't a kid now.

In light of the reason for yesterday's visit, he should beware of her, but it didn't seem to dim the effect she had on him. If he was not mistaken, she had not been indifferent to him either. And he was insane to be thinking along these lines. He had a widowed mother and four younger siblings to take care of—and electric lines to get constructed to many homes, including that of his own family.

A glance at his watch told him he was making good time, so he yielded to an impulse and turned onto the road that went past the school. About a mile down the road, he parked in the open space alongside the building and slipped through the door.

Miss Delaney stood with her back to the door, writing on the blackboard. He spotted a chair at the right of the doorway and slid silently onto it. From everything he had heard on visits home over the years, Jolene was a good teacher. Could the little sister be that capable? He did a visual scan of the students and located Wesley in a desk near the back of the row to his right.

When the teacher turned and spotted him, her eyes widened in recognition. She started to speak, but he shook his head and placed a finger across his lips to signal that she should continue and ignore him. After a brief pause she went on with the lesson.

He studied the room with an eye to wiring logistics. Schools, churches, filling stations, grain elevators and stores were given priority for getting electricity. He did a quick assessment and returned his attention to the classroom activities.

He found that he liked the way Miss Delaney interacted with the students. She presented the facts without chasing rabbits and corrected mistakes without scolding or talking down to the children. And she treated each student equally.

He knew the moment Wesley detected his presence. The boy had made a furtive move that bespoke mischief, but when he turned in his seat and spotted Gavin, he jerked back around.

Gavin's gut rolled. The young teacher truly did have her hands full with an angry young man. His respect for her went up a notch as he realized she had handled things herself a long time before coming to talk to Mom. He observed for a few more minutes. Then he put his gloves back on and slipped out the door. Now he had to deal with Mr. Delaney.

Irene relaxed when their silent guest left. Being watched had made her nervous, but she took it as a positive that Gavin Mathis had taken time to drop in and check on Wesley.

When afternoon recess time arrived, she went outside and watched the children play. Back inside, they spent the last part of the day rehearsing for next week's Christmas program. She went home exhausted and looking forward to having a few days off to celebrate the birth of Jesus and relax with her family.

The next week was hectic with last-minute Christmas preparations. Irene's dad, Sam, cut a cedar tree and

brought it to the school for the students to decorate. Then
they spent extra time practicing their play and songs for
Thursday night. When Thursday night finally arrived,
Irene dismissed the students an hour early so they could
go home and do their chores, eat and return for the program. She stayed at the school, ate the sandwich she had
brought and put a few final touches to the staging and
decorations the children had created. Then she changed
into the brightest dress she owned, a red one with a white
collar and cuffs. She combed her hair and left it down
instead of coiling it into a bun on the back of her head
as she wore it for teaching.

An hour before the start of the program, cars and wagons began to arrive. The children each went about their
assigned tasks. Wesley Bozeman and Eddie Dawson met
families at the door and took the lanterns brought by each
party. Then they hung them from the hooks on the walls,
where they would light the room most evenly.

Lord, please be in control. Help me not be nervous.

When the families had been seated in the desks normally occupied by the students, Irene went to the front
center of the room. Heart pitter-pattering, she licked her
dry lips and greeted the families of her students. Then
a calm came over her. When she finished speaking, she
moved to the side of the room, where she could oversee
the students.

They had erected a manger scene in a front corner of
the room. Drawings of sheep and donkeys were tacked
to the wall on one side of it. Judy Goodman, one of the
older students, stood to one side of the scene and began to
read the Christmas story. She had read only a few words
when the door opened and Gavin Mathis entered. Irene's
heart did a strange little thump as her eyes followed him
to a spot along the wall where he leaned back to watch.

Costumed children moved into the scene to portray the characters in the story. As the shepherds stepped into place, the lantern hanging on the wall behind the manger grew dim, flickered and went out.

Judy continued to narrate, speaking from memory, as she could no longer see her Bible. She slowed and came to a halt.

Irene took the lantern from the hook nearest her and carried it over to replace the one that had gone out. She had just hung it up and turned away when it also flickered and the flame died. Around the room other lanterns did the same—until all of them were dark.

"What should we do, Miss Delaney?" Judy whispered in the dark.

"Stay right where you are and wait quietly."

Gavin squelched the foreboding in his gut and edged his way to the door. He slipped outside, trotted to his car and found the flashlight he kept under the seat. Then he turned it on and went back inside. He could hear people shuffling around in the dark, taking the lanterns from the walls. From the front of the room Miss Delaney's calm voice kept the children under control while the adults handled the lighting problem.

When he arrived with the small light, several men gathered around him.

"Mine's not got any kerosene in it," one of them sputtered loudly. "It was full when we left home."

"Same here," another said.

All eight lanterns had been full of fuel but were now empty.

"What in tarnation!" an angry parent shouted. "Let me get my hands on the rascal who did this. I'll put his lights out."

"Calm down, Charles. Let's see if we can find some kerosene so the kids can finish. Then we'll deal with the troublemaker." A mother's softer voice soothed her husband.

"I have a jug in my wagon," someone said. "I'll get it."

Gavin accompanied the man to his wagon with the flashlight. Within minutes, they returned and filled the lanterns. Miss Delaney had the children begin the program again, and they presented it in its entirety without further mishap.

When the program ended, the applause was exuberant.

Elliott Markham, president of the school board, stood beside his seat. "Thank you, Miss Delaney, for an excellent job and the way you handled everything tonight."

He marched to the front of the room and addressed the audience in a less joyous tone. "Now I want to know who emptied those lamps."

Chapter 2

His sixth sense kicking in, Gavin's gaze angled over to where Wesley had been sitting. The boy had just slithered out of his seat and headed for the door, his little brother close behind him. All eyes in the room gravitated to them.

As the two boys slipped out the door, Gavin got up and followed them, not caring at that point who watched or what conclusions they drew. He had nothing but instinct telling him the boys were guilty, or at least involved.

He hated that his younger half brothers had no male role model. It was a role he didn't particularly relish for himself, but it seemed he was being thrust into it. He caught up with the rascals at the corner of the school building. "Where you going, guys?"

Two heads whipped around as the boys skidded to a halt. He couldn't see their eyes, but their startled reaction signaled guilt—and resentment.

"Since when do I have to tell you when I gotta go to the outhouse?" Wes's voice rang with belligerence.

Gavin folded his arms across his chest and stood firm, blocking their way.

"I thought you was going to get the kerosene," Lonnie blurted.

Wes faced his little brother. "You little…" He clamped his mouth shut.

"Just get it," Gavin ordered. "We'll talk about consequences later."

Wes shrank back for a moment, but then he gave an angry huff and spun on his heel. He stalked angrily to Gavin's truck, of all places, and reached over the side. He lifted out a big gas can and plunked it down on the ground at Gavin's feet. "It was just a joke. Good grief, can't anybody take a joke around here?"

"It isn't funny when you deliberately mess up a program the whole school has worked on for weeks. And you could be accused of stealing kerosene."

Gavin softened his tone a bit as he recognized fear settling into the boy's tense body. "There's nothing wrong with an occasional joke, but there's a point when too much is a mistake. Everyone makes mistakes sometimes. Then they have to face up to what they've done and make it right if they can. Are you ready to face up to this one?"

"You're not my dad," Wes muttered. He shook off his younger brother's hand, which had crept over into his.

Gavin braced himself and drew a deep breath. "No, I'm not. But we share a mom, and I know it hurts her when any of us get in trouble. I lost my dad when I was younger than you were when Roy died. I didn't have an older brother—or half brother—around to help bail me out of my messes. You do, if you're willing to work with me."

Behind them the schoolhouse door opened. Elliott Markham's form filled the opening.

"What'll it be?"

Wes glanced back at the board president and drew a shaky breath. Then he headed toward the building. Gavin and Lonnie followed him.

Wes handed the can of kerosene to Mr. Markham. "Here's the kerosene. I didn't steal it. I just wanted to play a joke, but I guess it wasn't a good idea. Sorry."

The board president closed the door and faced them. His eyes traveled to Gavin and the smaller boy at his side. His hard expression relaxed a bit.

Even facing Mr. Markham, Gavin couldn't keep his gaze from returning to the front of the room where the flickering light from the lanterns glinted off Miss Delaney's black hair and red dress. He normally didn't pay a lot of attention to what women wore or how they looked, yet he had an unexplainable awareness of this one.

"All right, since you've returned the kerosene, I won't call the marshal."

Mr. Markham's words pulled Gavin's attention back to the matter at hand.

"But I'll be checking with Miss Delaney about your behavior after this. If there's any more trouble, you'll answer to me," he added in a tone of barely constrained anger.

Good. Gavin felt a bit guilty for welcoming the board president's warning. But Wes would pay more attention to him than his own family, particularly a half brother who hadn't been around until recently.

Irene rolled pieces of chicken in flour and placed them in the skillet of hot grease, enjoying freedom from the stresses of the past week. As of today's early dismissal after their classroom Christmas party, she had survived her first half year of teaching. She jumped back as hot grease spattered onto the long sleeve of her blue cotton dress.

A lump came to Irene's throat as she wiped the spot with a dish towel, recalling last night's apology from Wesley Bozeman and the role Gavin Mathis undoubtedly had played in it.

The sound of a motor drew her to the window. To her surprise, the object of her thoughts parked his truck and came striding toward the house. With a fringe of sandy hair drawing a line beneath his hat, dark eyebrows and a five-o'clock shadow, Gavin's good looks made her heart do an acrobatic somersault. She watched him wade through the four inches of snow that had fallen during the night, his dark pants and black coat looking surprisingly fresh for so late in the day. When he got to the front steps, she wiped her hands on a dish towel and hurried to the door.

Gavin's hand was raised to knock when she opened it. He withdrew the hand and snatched his hat from his head. "Miss Delaney?"

"Yes, but you can call me Irene." She stepped back and widened the opening, a flutter tickling her stomach. "Please come in."

He entered the room and pushed the door shut behind him. He stopped on the protective rug that lay before the door. "Don't want to let that cold air in here." His voice was deep and smooth, but the way he fidgeted with his hat indicated discomfort. His eyes scanned the room beyond her, taking in the high ceiling and dark woodwork and then pausing for a moment on her upright piano, which sat across the room from the fireplace next to an inner wall.

"If you're looking for Dad, I'll have to go get him. He's outside doing chores."

"Oh, no," he said, sounding a bit relieved. "It's you I

wanted to see. I was on my way home from work and thought I would stop by to discuss Wesley's behavior. Has Mr. Markham spoken to you?"

Irene shook her head and indicated the sofa facing the fireplace. "Please have a seat."

He glanced down at his wet work boots. "I don't want to track across your floors."

Irene grinned and pointed at the chair near the door. She picked up the extra rug from the hearth and positioned it between the rug on which he stood and the chair. "Sit there, then. I'll be right back." She hurried to the kitchen and moved the sizzling skillet from the center of the stove to the edge, where it was not so hot.

"Sorry, I have chicken frying," she said when she returned, taking a seat in the rocker facing him. "To answer your question, no, Mr. Markham hasn't talked to me."

"He said he'll be checking with you about Wes from time to time to make sure he isn't still pulling stunts that involve stealing or harm to others. I'd appreciate it if you would let me know as well if there's more trouble. I also wondered how much you know about his home situation. Not that anything justifies his causing trouble," he added, working his hat in a circle by its brim.

Irene had lived here all her life and knew their neighbors for miles around. "I know his dad died about a year ago, and he's the oldest of the four children. That is, not counting you."

He nodded. "Things have been tough for Mom. That's why I came back here as soon as the company had a job opening for me in the area. Wes is a trial to her and the girls. I think he'll be okay when he grows up a bit, but I'm afraid his jokes will cause harm before then."

"I'll let you know if he gets out of hand." As the words left her mouth, the sound of the back door opening drew their eyes toward the kitchen. Moments later Irene's dad appeared in the doorway, a full milk pail in each hand. He scowled when he saw Gavin.

"Why you back here?" he barked. "Don't you understand when a man says no?"

Irene looked back and forth between her dad and Gavin. "No about what?"

"About hooking us up to that electric line they want to bring through here," Sam growled. "It's not worth all the expense."

Gavin's jaw tightened. "I didn't come to see you again, Mr. Delaney. I stopped to talk to your daughter about a school matter. We've talked, so I'll be running along."

He got up and opened the door.

A sense of loss washed over Irene as Gavin left. She spun to face her dad, but he had gone to put the milk buckets on the kitchen table. She marched after him, tears threatening. "You didn't tell me you talked to Gavin."

"He was by here last week." He picked up a white cloth and folded it in half.

"What do you mean, it's not worth the expense?" she nearly shouted. "Don't you know I would give almost anything for a washing machine and refrigerator?"

He looked up from wrapping the cloth over one side of a bucket and studied her face.

"I'll pay the sign-up fee," she said, swiping at her eyes.

His jaw dropped, as did the straining cloth. He set the bucket down. "I guess I didn't realize how much you want electricity." The muscle in his jaw twitched. "The sign-up fee is only the beginning of the expenses."

Irene's hopes fell, but she couldn't let it go. "Do you know how much the rest would be?"

"I did some checking." Regret now laced his tone. "We would have to get the house wired. Even if I joined a group wiring plan, the cost would still be fifty-five dollars. Then we would have to buy materials and hire men to do the work. I heard that manufacturers working with the REA are putting out lighting packages that sell for about eighteen dollars. I'm sorry, but all that together is more than I can scrape together right now."

Desperation drove Irene. "Could you find half of it if I pay the other half?"

He shook his head but seemed less certain. "I might manage half, but how in the world would you pay the rest? You barely make enough at the school to keep yourself dressed and run that car you bought last summer."

Irene chewed her lower lip, thinking fast. She played for her uncle's gospel quartet, but she didn't get paid for that. Another thought occurred. "I'll give piano lessons," she declared in a rush. "Pearl still has a few students, but her fingers are so crippled with arthritis that she has hinted for me to take over for her. I owe her so much, but I didn't agree to do it, because I'm so busy with my new teaching job. But I'll find the time somehow."

"That'll take forever," he pointed out.

Irene did some rapid calculations in her head. "How soon would everything have to be paid?"

He rubbed his chin. "I'm not sure. They just want the sign-up fee now. The wiring would probably have to be done around spring."

"I can do it. I will do it," she amended. Another thought formed. "Jolene sends articles to *Grit* magazine and gets paid for them. I can do that, too."

As her dad's eyes bored into her, she felt she could hear the wheels turning in his brain. She held her breath and waited. "All right, sweetheart," he said after several long moments. "Pay the sign-up fee. Then we'll figure out how to pay for the rest."

Elated, Irene ran to the stove and moved the skillet completely off the heat. She hurried to her bedroom and grabbed her coat and purse, putting the coat on as she raced out the door into the early sunset of winter.

Thankfully, the car started right off, not having sat in the cold long enough to freeze up. She put it in gear and took off down the road. Gavin lived only a mile and a half from them. She made a right turn halfway between her house and the Blake farm and was barreling down the hill toward the valley where the Bozeman family lived when she spied a truck parked at the side of the road. A man hunkered on the ground next to the right rear tire. It was Gavin.

Irene pulled in behind the truck and parked.

Gavin tightened the nut on the tire he had just put in place and looked back at the car. Irene Delaney emerged and came toward him at a brisk pace. She carried her purse and was opening it as she walked.

"Here's the five-dollar sign-up fee," she blurted without preliminary, skating to a stop on the snow-packed road. She pulled the money from her purse and poked her arm toward him.

He got up and brushed the snow from the knees of his dark pants. "I'll give you a receipt. Can you wait a couple of minutes while I write it?" he asked as he took the money.

"Of course." She smiled a little, and her gaze held for several seconds before she glanced down. Something in her timid manner touched him. Warmth spread through him.

What was he thinking? He knew better than to mix business and pleasure, no matter how intrigued he was by those shiny black eyes and that glossy black hair. She looked young—way too young—and pretty in her black coat and shoes.

He tossed the ruined tire in the back of the truck and went around to lean inside the cab and get the receipt pad from the seat, acutely aware of her gaze on him as he picked it up and wrote. He was certain he could feel her dark eyes beaming right through his heavy coat.

He turned around. "I remember you as a little tomboy." Now, why had he made such a comment?

"Still am," she responded easily.

He signed the form and tore it off the pad. "You don't look much like your sister," he said as he handed it to her.

"Jolene's more like Dad. I look like our mom. Of course, Jolene took care of me for so long after Mom died that she seems like my mom," she added with a shrug.

"You must be freezing."

Irene shook her head. "No more than you. It looks like you need to get home and fix a tire, and I have to get back to cooking supper. Thanks for this." She held up the receipt as she backed away. She wore a happy smile that held him immobile as she executed a backward wave and returned to her car.

The holiday vacation from school passed in a whirlwind. Jolene insisted that Christmas dinner be at her and Riley's house while she wasn't teaching and had more time to prepare. All Riley's family members who still lived in the area attended.

Irene and her dad had put what money they had saved toward the expenses of getting electricity rather than buying gifts beyond the candy they'd already bought.

The day after Christmas Irene talked to Pearl Harris and agreed to accept her piano students as soon as school resumed in January.

The morning of January 3 was so bitter cold that her car wouldn't start. Irene heated two kettles of water. Her dad poured one of them over the radiator and the other onto the motor to warm them. Once the car sputtered to life, Irene climbed in and spread a blanket over her lap to keep from freezing.

White puffs formed before her mouth as she parked at the school and got out. She hurried inside, where Zada Lonigan was struggling to get a fire going in the stove.

"Let's put a few more pine knots in there." Irene gathered a handful from the smaller wood box. Together they stuffed the kindling in between the bigger pieces of wood and watched in satisfaction as they burst into flames. Minutes later children began to arrive, bundled in their warmest clothing, their cheeks and noses bright red from the cold.

Other than everyone struggling to keep warm and Irene having to reorient the students to their study routine after the long break, the day went without incident. Until just before dismissal time.

"Wesley, please sit down. I haven't dismissed everyone yet," she said when the boy went to the side of the room and grabbed his coat from a hook.

He turned and glared at her, then continued to shrug into the coat. "It's time to go."

"It's time to go when I say so," she responded firmly. "Return to your seat and wait until the entire class is dismissed."

Anger flashed across his face, and he turned as if to stalk out of the building. Then he paused and returned to his seat. But he sat with his arms folded across his chest, glowering.

Some of the tension drained from Irene. She may have won this little battle of wills, but it would not be the last challenge. He was right about the time, but he had to understand that he did not run the classroom—and that he could not intimidate her.

"Okay, class, you may go now." She went to stand by the door while they got their coats. Some of the younger ones required help with their boots and mittens.

Irene's heart ached when she noted the ragged condition of the coats of the Holman sisters, Thelma, Velma and Selma. She had hoped they would show up with better ones after Christmas. She would talk to Jolene and her best friend, Callie. If anyone could help, they were the ones.

As all the students exited but Zada, Irene heard a motor. She looked out the door to see Gavin Mathis drive up to the building and park. She put on her coat and went out onto the step, pleased to see the Bozeman kids getting into his truck rather than having to walk home in the frigid cold. The girls sat on the laps of the boys in order for all of them to fit into the cab.

To Irene's surprise, Gavin did not drive away immediately. Instead he said something to his younger siblings and got out of the truck.

"How did the day go?" he asked as soon as he got to the steps. As usual, his handsome good looks distracted her.

Irene hesitated, not sure whether to mention the minor incident. But he deserved the truth. She gave him a brief account of Wesley's test of her authority.

"What do you suggest Mom or I do?" he asked when she finished.

"Nothing. I'll deal with him if you'll support me."

He eyed her closely before answering. "If you keep me informed on a regular basis."

Irene saw no problem with that. Rather, she welcomed his continued interest. She nodded. "I'll let you know if he causes trouble." Of course, she would judge whether the trouble warranted such contact.

"Thank you." He touched his hat and turned.

Irene watched him go back to his truck. Although she and Gavin Mathis were not close friends, they seemed to be developing a healthy respect for one another.

The next day Irene wondered how Wesley would act and respond to her. Her fears were soon put to rest. He ignored her, but he seemed in surprisingly good spirits around the rest of the students. Unfortunately, those good spirits rose as the day progressed.

A spate of giggles made her turn from the blackboard and scan the class. All eyes were focused on Wesley. He had put something, probably sticks, behind his ears to prop them out from his head. With his face contorted, he did look funny. But it had classroom work at a standstill.

"Wesley, why don't you come up here in front of the class, where we can all see you better, and look funny so we can all have a good laugh together."

His clown face disappeared, to be replaced by a frown.

"Come on." She beckoned with an index finger. "Let's get the laughing session done so we can get on with our work."

Wesley swiveled his head to look at the faces around the room, all locked on him. For a moment Irene thought he would refuse and bolt from the room, but he slowly got to his feet. Then he stomped loudly to the front.

"Now show us your funny face to go with the elephant ears."

He rolled his eyes, then did as she said. But only for a few moments. It suddenly didn't seem so funny to him or anyone else. A few smiles appeared, but Irene suspected they were more from amusement at his predicament than his funny looks.

"Okay, you may sit down," she said when he stared at her, his expression a mixture of discomfort and anger. "Now everyone exchange papers and we'll check the answers to your arithmetic problems."

"Wes doesn't have his done, Miss Delaney."

The announcement came from Wesley's seatmate, who traded papers with him regularly.

"Exchange with Maggie, then." She looked at Wesley, now truly exasperated with him. "You may stay after school to finish your work."

An hour later the room had emptied of students except for Wesley and Zada, both eighth graders. Irene returned to her desk from seeing the other students out and marked papers while Wesley worked furiously at his desk and Zada did her janitorial work.

Minutes later Wesley came to her desk and tossed his paper onto it. "May I leave now?" His words were polite, but his tone was grudging.

Irene glanced at the paper. "You may."

"I'm done, Miss Delaney," Zada announced shortly after Wesley left. "See you in the morning." She got her coat and went out the door.

Irene gathered her things and put on her coat to leave. As she reached the door, a scream split the air outside the building.

Chapter 3

Irene propelled herself to the door and rushed outside. The sight before her sent anger firing through her. Wesley had a snake in his hand, and he was chasing Zada Lonigan around the schoolyard with it. Irene ran down the steps. "Wesley, stop that this minute. Leave her alone."

No sooner had the words left her mouth than a motor sounded in the distance. Seconds later a truck pulled up to the school, driven by Gavin Mathis.

Sparing only a glance at the truck, Irene ran toward the two students. "Wesley! Zada!"

Wesley paused and looked around. When he recognized the truck, he came to an abrupt halt and shoved the snake down inside the front of his coat. At the same time, Zada darted into Irene's open arms. Irene held the trembling girl to her chest.

"What's going on?" Gavin asked as he approached, his voice sharp. He aimed a suspicious look at Wesley, who had adopted his usual air of innocence.

Zada raised her head and peered over at Gavin. "Wesley knows I'm afraid of snakes. He has one, and he chased me with it." She shuddered.

The grim expression on Gavin's face turned thoughtful, his brows scrunched together. "In January?"

Zada backed away from Irene, frowning. Then her expression did a slow transformation as she comprehended the unlikelihood of a snake being around in this cold weather. Fists clenched, she lunged toward Wesley and grabbed his arm.

Acting quickly, Gavin got to them and pulled them apart. Once he had a couple of feet between the two, he looked down at the tail protruding from Wesley's coat. He pulled it out. What had looked like a snake at a distance proved to be a piece of thick dark rope with eyes and rattlesnake markings painted on it.

He shook his head in exasperation. "If you spent half as much time actually working as you do at working on silly jokes, it would be incredible what you could accomplish."

Wesley glared and jerked his arm away. "Why do you have to be such a grouch and spoil everybody's fun? And you don't tell me what to do."

A muscle jerked in Gavin's jaw. "Everybody is not having fun. It's only you, and you're causing hurt and unhappiness for others in order to have it. As for telling you what to do, I'm telling you to get in there and wait for me. You can discuss it with Mom when we get home." He jabbed a finger in the direction of his truck.

The boy folded his arms to balk, but when Zada made another grab for him and Irene held her back, he huffed in anger and stomped away.

"I need to get home," Zada said when Wesley was in the truck. "Zona will be worried about me if I'm any later."

"Okay, run along." Irene knew Zada was right. Mrs. Lonigan cowered beneath the rule of her domineering husband. And she pretty much left running of the household to sixteen-year-old Zona, who had quit school last year when their brothers, Troy and Chuckie, had gone to prison. Irene figured it was only a matter of time until Mr. Lonigan landed in serious trouble with the law— rather, more trouble.

"I meant to ask how the day went," Gavin said when Zada was out of hearing range. "But now I'm afraid to ask." He grimaced and rolled his eyes upward. "I assume you kept Wes late."

Irene put her arms around herself as her teeth chattered from the cold. "I'm afraid so." She gave him a quick report of Wes's transgressions.

Gavin heaved a deep sigh. "I hate to add to Mom's troubles, but I have to tell her he's still acting ornery. I can't come home and start playing the heavy when the kids hardly know me. She'll have to be the one to discipline him. All I can do is help her when she asks."

"I'll continue to pray for Wesley," Irene promised.

He shrugged. "If you think it'll help."

She tipped her head. "You don't believe in God?"

"Oh, I believe in God. I just doubt He's interested in these little matters. I haven't been to church much in recent years."

"Why did you quit?" She was curious in spite of the cold.

"Mom married Bozo…uh, Roy Bozeman when I was a kid. He went to church with her when they were courting, but after they married, he quit going. He said holy things in public but talked and acted different in private. He was a hypocrite and didn't take good care of Mom. God let her down."

Irene shook her head. "You were young and didn't realize that God didn't let her down. Only Roy did that."

He shrugged again. "If you say so. Well, I have to go." He turned and left.

"He was quiet today, almost subdued," Irene said when Jolene asked about Wesley's behavior the next day. Jolene knew the boy better than anyone, having taught him from the time he started school.

Jolene huffed and pressed the iron into her husband's shirt with such force that Irene feared she would burn it. "His mother probably gave him a whipping. She's had to deal with too much. That shiftless man she married didn't help her with anything. He spent more time hanging out in town with his cronies than on the farm and worked Gavin like a farmhand. Nell took care of the kids and the place, too. Having Gavin back home has to be a real blessing to her. I'm glad he's showing an interest in Wesley. And you."

Irene shook her head in disbelief. "You're imagining things."

Jolene grinned, undaunted, and put the shirt on a hanger. "Don't think so. He's showing up too often to only be interested in his little brother's behavior."

"Even if I were interested in a man, he's too old for me. And you've told me plenty of times that I'm too tomboyish and busy to ever think about getting hitched." Irene avoided the word *married*. "If you want to stay my sister and best friend, you'll drop this line of talk. Do you or Callie know where I can get hold of some coats for the Holman girls? Theirs are ragged and too small for them."

A frown puckered Jolene's brow. "They didn't get new ones this year? I had hoped they would. Theirs were in terrible shape last year. I'll talk to Callie tomorrow. Between us maybe we can come up with three coats. Would you like us to see that they get them so you don't have to take them to school where the other children will know?"

Jolene understood from experience how embarrassed the girls might feel at having their poverty emphasized by receiving clothing in front of their classmates. It also could cause jealousy among the other students if the girls got something they didn't or could be seen as favoritism. Before Callie Blake married Trace Gentry, she and Jolene had started a food-and-clothing swap in town. They still had stuff stored in the back of the Gentry car dealership, but they didn't open it regularly in the winter. "I appreciate the help. Thanks."

"Have you decided what you're going to do when the school year ends?"

Jolene's change of topic caught Irene off guard. "I guess I'll take some more piano students," she said offhandedly. A full-time job involving music seemed more impossible all the time. "I've written an article for the *Grit* paper. Will you read it over and see if you think it's good enough to send to them?"

Jolene put the iron down. "You have it with you?"

"Of course." Irene took it from her bag and handed it to her sister. "I have piano students due in a few minutes, so I need to run."

"I'll bring this back to you tomorrow."

The next day, Friday, Gavin got off work too late to stop by the schoolhouse and check on Wes on his way home. And see Miss Delaney. He got out of the truck and headed to the house. Mom had been coughing last night. He hoped she was feeling better.

"Where's Wesley?" he asked when he stepped through

the door. His mother and the girls were putting supper on the table and his mom did seem better.

"He'll be in soon. He's running a little late with chores."

Gavin took off his coat and hat and faced his mother. "Did he have to stay after school?"

Mom shook her head. "No, and he cut some extra wood before going to the barn."

"So he had a good day." It was half statement, half question.

She nodded, wiping her hands on her apron. "I think so."

"He didn't get in any trouble," Jenny volunteered, pausing with a plate in her hand. "Of course, that doesn't mean he won't be back up to his old tricks come Monday."

Mom's mouth tightened. "He better not."

Gavin hoped not, too. He hated for Mom to have to wear out Bozo's old belt. "How are you feeling?"

She shrugged. "Tired."

"I'll wash the dishes so you can rest after supper, Mom," Cassie volunteered.

"I'll dry," added Jenny.

The girls seemed extra helpful tonight. Gavin appreciated their willingness to help Mom, but he couldn't help but wonder if they had more on their minds.

Wesley came through the door just then, carrying a milk bucket in one hand and an ax in the other. "This thing's dull," he said, setting the ax next to the doorway and the milk bucket on the cabinet. "I'll sharpen it after supper." He seemed in a good mood.

"Wash up and get to the table," Mom ordered as she set a platter of sliced bread next to the one of ham.

Within minutes, they had taken their places. As soon

as Mom had said the blessing, they began to pass the ham, fried potatoes and gravy. Gavin found he was hungrier than he had realized.

Cassie reached for the bread. "Gavin, will you take us to the church in town tomorrow night? I sure would like to go."

"Me too," Jenny chimed in.

Gavin looked from one girl to the other. "Why do you want to go to a church other than your own?"

"Because they're having a gospel singing group from Georgia," Cassie explained.

"I've been hearing about it," Mom confirmed. "It's a family by the name of LeFevre. Everyone says they're real good."

"Do you want to go?"

She inhaled heavily. "I wouldn't mind, if I feel up to it."

His gaze traveled to Wes. "How about you?"

Wes swallowed quickly. "Sure. A lot of the kids from school will probably be there."

And he would like a Saturday-night outing. "We couldn't get everybody in the cab of my truck. It's awful cold to ride in the back."

"I don't mind," Lonnie piped up as he spread butter on his bread.

"Me either," Wes insisted. "We'd hunker down behind the cab so the wind wouldn't hit us so hard."

Gavin looked back at Mom. "If you feel up to it, then I guess we'll go."

As soon as they finished supper, Mom and the girls started to clear the table. "You go on and rest. We'll do this," Cassie told Mom.

She didn't argue but went to lie down, which told Gavin she was feeling very poorly. "I'll sharpen that ax if you guys have homework you want to do." He got up to get it.

"We don't *want* to do it, but Mom says we have to do it at the beginning of the weekends and not leave it until Sunday nights," Cassie said with a grin. "How about a game of dominoes after we get done," she suggested to the other kids.

Gavin took a whet rock and the ax to the living room and settled into a chair. The sounds from the kitchen were pleasant. As soon as the dishes were done, the kids put the kerosene lamp in the center of the table and sat around it. When they finished their homework, they played a lively game of dominoes. Mom slept during the entire hour and a half. Then she got up and sent the kids to bed. "Morning comes early," she reminded them as usual.

When they were bedded down for the night, Mom settled in the rocker with a sigh. "This is peaceful," she said, leaning her head back and closing her eyes for a moment. Then she opened them and took her Bible from the small table at her side. "I've been trying to get back to some habits we used to have."

Gavin put the ax down and nodded at the Bible. "You mean like reading that? And going to church?"

A look of sadness—regret?—crossed her face. "I'm sorry to say I quit some things after I married Bozey. But I never stopped praying. The Bible says we should pray without ceasing. That's what kept me going when I got discouraged and wanted to quit everything."

"Bo...zey—" he caught himself before he could say *Bozo* "—wouldn't go to church with you, and you got tired of going alone."

"I got tired, period. And I was angry. Bozey wouldn't go to church with me like he promised when we were courting. Then the kids started coming, all close together. Next thing I knew, I had my hands so full with little ones that I gave up and quit going, too. The thing I hate most is what the situation did to you. Bozey never treated you fair."

"Don't fret about it, Mom. I was a big boy. I loved you, and I understood. We had been alone a long time, and you were lonely."

"You were only twelve when I married him," she protested. "You never should have been treated as less important than the other kids and made to work more than he did."

She gave him a pointed look. "For you the marriage was a mistake. But if I hadn't done it, I wouldn't have them." She jerked her head toward the part of the house where the kids slept. "I love them and can't imagine life without them."

He smiled. "I know that. Always did. And I knew you loved me. I love the kids, too." Bozo had never physically abused Gavin other than making him work all the time, but he had only tolerated him, never loved him.

Mom rubbed her eyes. "You were a good boy. You did whatever it took to keep him happy. But I know he's why you left home so young. I missed you."

"I missed you, too, Mom. But I needed to learn how to take care of myself."

"Now you've come back to take care of me and the kids when you should be taking care of a family of your own." She heaved another sigh. "I feel so guilty."

"There's no need. I have a job I like, and I enjoy being back. Besides, I can't have a family of my own until I find someone to have it with."

"I started taking the kids to church again after Bozey died," she said. "I lost my fellowship with the Lord for a long time, but never my relationship. That's restored now, but it breaks my heart that you lost your fellowship and never regained it. For that I'm truly sorry. I wish you would go to church with us."

Gavin got to his feet. "I'll think about it. I'm tired." He pulled her up and gave her a hug. "Don't stay up too late."

"I'll go back to bed soon as I read a little bit," she promised.

Gavin didn't drop off to sleep as he had thought he would. Instead he lay in bed with thoughts and images filling his mind. His mother's words about how she never stopped praying brought back Miss Delaney's statement that she would continue to pray for Wesley. Prayer seemed to be such a natural part of their lives. Miss Delaney would make someone a wonderful wife someday.

Why he should think of Irene Delaney in that context eluded him. Even if she should think of him in that way, he already had a family to take care of. He fought with his pillow, pounded it into place and flopped onto his side.

Twelve-year-old Cassie hung back and edged over next to Gavin as Mom and Jenny got into the truck. Then she made a hasty move toward him and wrapped her arms around his waist. "I'm glad you came home and I have you for a big brother," she said just loud enough for him to hear. "I worried at first that you wouldn't like us. But you're nice. And I love you," she added in a self-conscious rush. Then she ran to the truck and squeezed in next to Mom, who had insisted she felt like going to the singing.

Now what had brought that on? Gavin went around and opened the driver's door. Could Cassie have over-heard him and Mom talking last night? He hoped not. But if she had, no harm seemed to have come from it.

When they got to town, he gazed at the lights in the buildings they passed. The hardest thing about return-ing home had been the lack of electricity he had grown accustomed to in the city.

The church was well lit, and well attended, from the looks of the nearly full parking lot. "These must be some popular singers to draw a crowd like this," he commented.

The girls didn't bother to hide their fascination when they entered the building. Much larger than the country church they and their neighbors attended, this one had stained-glass windows along each side, high ceilings, and a huge auditorium that was nearly full and humming with talk and an air of excitement.

They had no sooner found a place to sit when the pastor led a song, prayed and introduced the musicians. "Ladies and gentlemen, let's welcome the LeFevre family, all the way from Atlanta."

The program that followed was a delightful array of singing and playing. The wife of one of the brothers, Eva Mae, played the piano with flair and style beyond anything Gavin had ever heard. She also sang and emceed for the group, something he knew to be rare in a world dominated by male groups.

After an hour of great singing, the group took a break, during which the ushers took up an offering. The pastor announced that a local group would sing a couple of songs to give the LeFevres time to catch their breath.

Gavin recognized Irene's uncle and aunt, Lee and Betty Brockman, and their friends Allen Palmer and Harry Dennison. But when the quartet began to sing, he couldn't believe his eyes and ears.

Chapter 4

Irene Delaney's playing was sheer artistry, as good as Mrs. LeFevre's, in Gavin's opinion. The little quartet did a fine job, but the flair of their accompanist definitely enhanced their performance.

Thinking back, Gavin remembered seeing her at the piano when she was a girl and he attended church with his mother. Irene had been a dainty thing, perched on that stool, her feet dangling several inches above the floor. But she didn't spend her time whirling the stool as the other kids did. She would sit there and pick out the melodies of hymns. By the time she was eight or nine, she had begun to play for services when Mrs. Harris, the regular pianist, had to be absent. But he had never imagined she would advance to the level he was hearing.

She deserves a stage of her own.

The two numbers the group sang ended all too quickly. When they left the stage, Gavin watched Irene make her

way to the pew where her family sat and slide in next to
her dad. He couldn't take his eyes off her.

An elbow nudged him. "Hey, the singing is up there."

He met Wesley's mischievous grin. The kids was entirely too observant. Probably came from being such a
prankster, always watching for opportunities and planning his moves.

"Mind your own business," he whispered into the
boy's ear. Then he faced forward and focused on the
guest musicians.

After the program ended, the pastor announced that
refreshments were available in the fellowship hall and invited everyone to stay. Gavin saw the gleam in the eyes
of the kids and didn't even try to suggest they skip the
goodies. His mother gave him a silent look of thanks.

As they followed the flow of people, the kids edged
away from him and Mom and joined a group of young
people.

Inside the large room that doubled as both a dining
and meeting room, tables along one wall were loaded
with cakes and cookies. Ladies served cups of coffee
and hot chocolate.

"I see you're finding plenty for your sweet tooth."

Gavin looked around to find Irene Delaney beside
him. She placed a platter of cookies that smelled of cinnamon on the table.

He grinned and added one of them to his already gen-
erously loaded plate. He had to do something to keep
from staring at her. Her shiny black hair and oval face
were lovely, but now that he had witnessed her talent, he
was truly entranced.

"I'll share if you'll join us," he said as they reached
the end of the line.

She gave him a cheerful little grin. "Why not?"

"I'll join my friends if you don't mind," his mother said as they glanced around for a place to sit. She went and set her plate down next to a friend.

Gavin led the way to the next table and deposited his plate on it. "Keep guard over this and I'll get drinks for us. You want coffee or hot chocolate?"

He saw a small twitch of Irene's lips, almost a smile. "Make it chocolate."

When he returned, Gavin noted that Wes had found himself a cozy spot at a table with Zada Lonigan and three younger girls who looked like sisters. He was teasing them all, but it was easy to see that the Lonigan girl was getting most of his attention.

"I'm beginning to think he likes Zada."

He sat and looked back at Irene. "I believe you're right. But he needs to learn how to treat a girl."

She grinned. "You mean in a way that doesn't involve phony snakes or hair pulling?"

He nodded. "Or exploding bullets. I hope he's ready to grow up enough to realize those aren't the kind of things that impress girls."

"He will." She said it with confidence and no hint of resentment over past incidents.

He swallowed the last of a cookie and tipped his head. "You seem suited to your job well enough, but why are you teaching when you have so much musical talent? Don't you want to do more with that?"

She put her mug down, her expression one of utter calm. "It's payback time."

He frowned. "Payback?"

She nodded. "I'm sure you know that my sister, Jolene, has been the teacher at Deer Creek School for years. But she was more of a mother to me than a sister. Our mother died when I was ten, and she was sick for years before that. Jolene took care of me from the time I was tiny, giving me all the love and care that our mother couldn't."

Gavin nodded. "I remember when your mother died."

"Jolene also supported my love of music. When I was a teenager, she sold her bicycle to buy me a piano. I decided then that someday I would find a way to help her. That chance came when she learned that she needed time off to have a baby. I was able to complete enough college courses and pass a teacher's examination for subjects I don't have enough college credits for just in time to step in as her replacement. The school board seemed happy to have me when Jolene explained her situation and my qualifications."

Gavin's mind ran ahead as he processed what she had told him. "So you're just teaching temporarily. Does that mean you have plans to do more with your music after your sister takes her job back?"

She made a little shoulder movement that wasn't quite a shrug. "That's my dream. But there aren't many opportunities for women in the gospel music field."

"Gospel music. You aren't interested in something more…uh…professional?"

Her face lost its glow. "I think I'm capable of playing whatever style of music I want, but I love gospel music, and it's a form of ministry. I think God wants me to use my talent for Him."

He raised a palm. "Sorry. I didn't mean anything negative about gospel music. I just…"

"I know what you meant," she assured him. "I also know how hard it will be. But Eva Mae LeFevre has done it. Why can't I? Of course," she added with a shrug, "the chances of my marrying a man who already has his own group the way she did is highly unlikely."

"Maybe you could marry a preacher who wants to take a revival team on the road."

Even as he said the teasing words, Gavin's insides twisted. For some reason, the idea of her marrying anyone—or leaving the area—struck a note of discord in him. "Do you play by ear or read music?"

She grinned. "Both. I started picking out melodies by ear as soon as I got big enough to climb onto the piano stool at the church. Then Pearl Harris took me under her wing."

"I remember. Wasn't Mrs. Harris the postmistress?"

Irene nodded. "She was also the church pianist for many years. But she had arthritis even when I was a kid. She came to the house one day and asked Dad and Jolene if they objected to her giving me lessons. In exchange, she asked that I come to her house once a week and do some cleaning tasks that had become difficult for her."

"It sounds like you made a good deal."

"It helped both of us." Her eyes returned to the table where Wesley and the girls sat. Slowly a smile worked its way across her face.

Gavin followed her gaze but saw nothing significant. "What's amusing?"

"Not amusing," she denied, breaking a cookie in half on his plate and taking one of the halves. "Just watching the pros at work."

He looked again. "All I see is your sister and her friend Callie joining the kids."

"Right. But the next thing you will see is them taking the Holman girls from the room." She popped a bite of cookie in her mouth.

No sooner had she said the words than he saw her prediction come true. "Where are they going, since you know so much?"

She chewed and swallowed the cookie. "I mentioned the girls' ragged coats to Jolene, and she promised to look for some. I'm sure she has them with her tonight. I'd better go help her." She got to her feet.

Gavin swallowed hard as he watched Irene walk away. The simple black dress she wore made her look elegant, but the red sash she had put around her waist added a touch of perkiness. Totally at ease, in her element, she followed her sister and the three girls from the room.

She had so much to admire. Beauty. Talent. And a love for those around her. He felt small in comparison. No point in dreaming about her, he reminded himself. She had the world at her feet, and dreams of leaving here. That excluded her from being the girl for him.

Midmorning the next Saturday, Irene peeked out the window when she heard a car pull in and stop at the house. She smothered a smirk and went to the living room, where her dad sat reading the weekly newspaper.

"You have company."

He read on for a second. Then his shaggy white brows raised in a startled movement of realization. "Is it that busybody widow?"

Irene smiled and nodded. "She's bearing goodies."

He shot to his feet. "Drat. I liked Bickford. But not enough to take on the woman he left behind." He grabbed his coat and hat.

"What shall I tell her?"

"I ain't here." He shoved his arms in his coat as he shot out the back door.

Irene snickered to herself and went to the door. She watched Juanita make her way up the steps, a cloth-covered basket dangling from her arm.

"Hello, Mrs. Tomlin," she greeted the woman as she stepped onto the porch.

"Hello yourself." Juanita took a quick breath. "Is Sam here?"

"He's out in the barn. I think he said one of the cows is sick." *He did earlier this morning, anyway.*

Her lips pursed. "Oh, fiddle. I brought him a rhubarb pie. I remember seeing him eat it at church dinners. And I canned a lot of it this past year."

Mrs. Tomlin, a strong little woman with a head of thick salt-and-pepper hair, had been their neighbor for years. She was the neighborhood gossip, and Irene had called her a chigger because of her ability to irritate. She no longer called her that—aloud. But the term came to mind right now.

The woman's husband, Bickford Tomlin, had died two years ago. At first Juanita had been grief stricken and had even stopped running from house to house with her gossipy tales. But about a year ago she had emerged from her mourning—and set her sights on Sam.

Juanita removed the pie from her basket and took it to the kitchen table. "I'll stop by and pick up the pan later."

Not if I can get it back to you first. "Thank you, Mrs. Tomlin. I'll tell Dad you left it just for him. I won't eat a bite of it."

"Oh, mercy, girl." She waved a hand in the air. "You should at least try a piece of it. It's delicious, if I do say so myself."

A thread of pity inched through Irene that the woman would so blatantly pursue her dad. Sam had been friends with Bickford but had never made a big secret of his dislike for the man's wife. Around his own family, that is. He had never aired his feelings beyond their walls.

"Well, I best be getting home," the lonely widow said. "I still have bread to bake."

Irene saw her to the door, wishing the woman's two grown children didn't live so far away in Kansas City. "I'll see you tomorrow," she said as Juanita headed back to her car.

Gavin's mother gazed across the breakfast table at him, her eyes lacking their normal luster. "Son, I don't feel up to taking the kids to church this morning. I know you don't go anymore, but I sure would appreciate it if you would take the kids for me today."

Gavin couldn't refuse her. "Tell them to get ready."

An hour later the sight of the white frame church in the clearing sparked memories. He had attended there with his parents when he was a baby, then with his mother after his dad died. That seemed like a long time ago now.

The wind had died down, but it had begun to snow. He hoped it didn't turn bad.

Wesley and Lonnie hopped out of the back of the truck and headed inside, probably not wanting to be seen with their sisters and big brother. The girls, wearing their best dresses and matching hair ribbons, seemed to take pride in walking beside Gavin.

They slipped into a pew near the back. He leaned over and whispered into Cassie's ear. "It's okay if you want to go sit with your friends."

She grinned up at him. "Thanks. We'll meet you at the truck after service."

As the girls moved to a pew to their right, several people got up and went to the choir. Irene Delaney, as expected, sat at the piano. She played a brief prelude, and then the song service began.

"Julie Hill was supposed to sing for us this morning,"

the pastor announced when the congregational hymns had ended and the choir members had returned to their pews. "But she's ill today. Mrs. Juanita Tomlin has kindly volunteered to sing for us."

The "special" music that followed was unlike anything Gavin had ever heard. The poor woman destroyed the melody and lyrics of an old hymn. She apparently equated volume with quality, judging by the howl she aimed at them.

At the piano, Irene deserved a medal for her effort at staying with the woman as she made a spectacle of herself. He was sure he could hear the inward sighs of relief when Mrs. Tomlin finished the song and went back to her pew.

The pastor also did a good job of keeping a straight face as he stepped to the pulpit to deliver his sermon. He held up a lightbulb.

"Ladies and gentlemen, we have heard lots of talk lately about the need for electricity in our rural areas, how it's exactly what farmers need to bring them out of the depression and give them equal standing with citizens who live in the towns and cities. But let us not forget that Jesus is the light of the world."

Gavin stared at the single bulb. Surely the pastor wasn't saying they didn't need electricity.

"Yes, we need electricity," the man continued. "Only the most affluent farmers and ranchers or those who live near town can get it. But as much as we need lights and power, let's never forget what Jesus said. 'I am the light of the world. Whosoever follows me will never walk in darkness but will have the light of life.'"

Looking around the room, Gavin watched heads nod and found that he recognized most of the people here. A few of their faces kindled memories of public behavior far from the calm expressions they now wore.

Who are you to judge others?

He swallowed a jolt of guilt. Yes, he had done things he would not want broadcast.

"As Christians we must let our light shine so that others may see our good works and glorify our Father in heaven. We are the light of the world."

The pastor's perspective intrigued Gavin. He had seen his job as important, but he had not thought much about God for years.

When the sermon ended and the pastor called on a deacon to pray, Gavin started to close his eyes. But movement near the door caught his attention. He glanced over just in time to see Wesley dart out the door.

Quietly he got up and followed.

At first Gavin didn't see Wes. He stood on the front steps of the church and surveyed the area around the building. Then a motion caught his eye over near a car. Miss Delaney's car. He headed that way.

Anger shot through him when he rounded the vehicle and found Wesley squatted next to a rear tire.

"You planning to spend the next year doing chores for your teacher?"

Startled, Wesley nearly fell backward when he recognized Gavin. His jaw dropped and his eyes widened in guilt.

The anger sent heat into Gavin's face. He watched wariness flit across the boy's features, and he took a deep breath to keep from exploding.

"I thought we had gotten past this kind of childish prank." He pointed a finger at his truck. "Get in there, and you'd better be there when I get back with the other kids. Be thinking about what you're going to tell Mom when we get home."

He spun on his heel and came up short when he found

himself face-to-face with Irene Delaney. He followed her gaze to Wesley behind him.

"I think you have a personal slave this week if you think you can trust him enough to do chores for you."

She nodded, her look on the boy as stern as his. "I can think of several jobs that need doing. Thank you for getting here in time to keep me from having a flat tire. Go on," she ordered Wesley. "I'll deal with you tomorrow."

In a burst of temper, Wesley whirled and stalked to the truck, visibly holding back from spewing the words Gavin was sure he would have said if his teacher had not been present.

"I'm sorry," Gavin said as soon as the boy got beyond hearing range. "I—"

"It's not your fault," she interrupted. "Don't feel like you have to take responsibility every time he does something. I'll deal with him at school. You deal with him at home. Fair enough?" She held out a hand.

He stared at it, thinking how good it felt to have her share his load. Her sunny smile sent a sweet thrill racing through him. He clasped her hand. "Deal."

Chapter 5

Irene shivered as she plodded across the yard to the porch. Moisture-laden wind whipped a miniature tornado of snow and dead leaves across the ground ahead of her. Her eyes watered and stung.

Once inside the house, she found that her dad had already started to build a fire in the cookstove. Without his help building fires in the fireplace and the kitchen stove in the mornings and evenings, Irene could not possibly have taught school and had meals ready at a decent hour.

"Thanks," she called over her shoulder as she hung her coat in the hall closet. "It's nice to have the kitchen already warming. How do you feel about pork chops for supper?"

"Like I could eat a dozen." Sam came through the doorway, a grin spread across his face. "I'll get the chores done quick as I can."

By the time he returned an hour later, Irene had fried

potatoes and the pork chops and had made gravy and biscuits.

"I raised you right," Sam said as they sat across the table from one another. He bowed his head and thanked the Lord for their food and Irene's cooking ability.

"Did you have a good day at school?" he asked after getting a few bites inside him.

Irene rolled her eyes. "School was fine. Recess was another matter."

Sam chuckled. "What did the Bozeman boy do this time?"

"He brought an umbrella to school and talked two younger boys into climbing up on top of the outhouse and parachuting off the roof. They nearly broke their legs."

"You should have made Wesley jump off that roof." He shook his head in commiseration. "It's hard to believe what that kid will do."

"His mother has him cleaning the barn at home, but I think she's about at her wits' end. I keep him busy at school. Or try to. But he still seems to have energy to burn and way too many crazy ideas."

They finished eating and cleared the table. As Irene washed the dishes, she heard a vehicle pull into the driveway. She peeked around the curtain to see Gavin Mathis coming across the yard. She went to the door and opened it within seconds of his knock.

"Sorry to bother you so late," he said. Shadows deepened the lines of fatigue in his face. "It's been a long day, and my partner has already gone home, but I wanted to stop by here and talk to your dad on my way home."

"He just went to the living room. I'm getting ready to take him some coffee. Would you like a cup?" She stepped back and opened the door farther.

Something in his manner, the way his eyes darted to

where she had told him her dad was, conveyed discomfort or nervousness.

"I could use a hot drink," he said, stepping inside the house.

Irene got him a mug while he took off his galoshes. "I'll put it here." She set it on the table next to a rocker.

He crossed the room and picked up the mug, cradling it in his hands as if to warm them. Then he took a long swallow and folded himself into the chair. His gaze lingered on her as she brought her own cup and sat in the chair facing him. The admiring sweep of his eyes sent a reluctant thread of excitement through her.

Sam reached over and turned off the radio. Then he leaned back in his overstuffed chair. "You look like a young man with something on his mind."

Face taut, Gavin raked a hand through his hair. His Adam's apple bobbed. Irene's stomach muscles tightened, sensing that whatever he had to say would not be pleasant to her dad.

He drew a long breath. "As you know, the rural electric movement is making good progress, but some snags have to be worked out along the way."

"I don't like the sound of this," Sam growled, sitting forward in his chair.

Gavin hesitated and then continued. "The REA did not approve use of funds to purchase rights-of-way over farmlands. So we need you to sign an easement for us to run poles across your property."

Irene watched the color rise in her dad's face. His mouth fell open slightly, and his eyes blazed with angry fire. He raised a finger and jabbed it in the air toward Gavin.

"First you people come around peddling your co-op idea and get our womenfolk to get behind it and put pressure on us. Then you hit us up for five dollars to sign up. Now you're asking us to give you a strip of our land. I don't believe the nerve of you people." His voice had risen to a bellow as he spoke.

"I know it's a lot to ask—"

"It's too much to ask." Sam cut him off. "You tell your bosses that I'm not signing any easement, and I want my sign-up fee back."

Irene sat and listened in horrified silence, absorbing the implications of her dad's uncharacteristic explosion. He rarely yelled or lost his temper. But since the REA had been formed and the countryside had grown excited about getting electricity, he had become a skeptic. Irene didn't understand his resistance.

Unlike her dad, she welcomed the changes that electricity would bring to those who got it. She couldn't wait to have lights and a refrigerator in place of the icebox that had to have a fresh block of ice in it way too often in order to keep their milk and butter cool. It made her angry that Dad could not grasp that. It also bothered her that the REA had not planned better.

Gavin got to his feet and strode to the door. He picked up his galoshes and left without taking time to put them on.

Irene watched him go, glad the discussion was over but irate about the results. Unable to speak to her dad without shouting or crying, she got up and practically ran into her room and locked the door.

She flung herself onto the bed and let the tears come. Maybe she should just pack her clothes and move to town. She could get a room at the hotel or in the private residence of a lonely widow. She would miss the farm, the only home she had ever known, but she would have lights and appliances.

A light tap sounded at the door. She ignored it and rolled over.

The week passed in strained silence. Irene came home from school each day and set to work on supper. During the meals, she and her dad hardly spoke, the atmosphere brittle between them. As soon as they finished eating Friday evening, Irene put on her coat and headed for the door.

"You going to Jolene's?"

Irene paused just long enough to say, "No, I'm going to see Rayona," and moved on.

Once she got the car started, it took only a few minutes to drive the two miles to town. Rayona Mitchell, her best friend from high school, still lived with her parents on the south side of town near where they owned and operated the local movie theater.

"What's wrong?" Rayona asked as soon as she opened the door after Irene's knock.

The depression that had dogged Irene ever since Tuesday night eased a bit at her friend's instant sympathy.

"Dad backed out of getting electricity."

"Oh, no." Rayona pulled her inside and wrapped comforting arms around her. "That's a tough blow. I know how hard you have to work and how excited you were when he signed up."

She drew back and studied Irene, as if gauging how to help her. "I know just what you need. Mom and Dad have already gone to the theater, and I have to be there in a few minutes to usher. Go with me. A night at the movies will be the perfect escape for you. We'll have time to visit when I'm between duties."

The Mitchells all had jobs in their family-run business. Mrs. Mitchell was the cashier and Mr. Mitchell the projectionist. Rayona's brother, Jay, ran the concessions, and Rayona ushered and helped wherever needed. They all swept floors, cleaned restrooms and scraped gum off the seats.

"I can't just sit around while you work. I'll help if you'll give me a task."

Rayona grinned. "You can help me and Jay, whoever gets the busiest and needs an assistant. Don't bother taking off your coat. I'll get mine."

Her friend was right. The bustling Friday-night theater atmosphere provided a temporary reprieve from her depressed state. Irene divided her time between bagging popcorn and helping usher. At seven o'clock Rayona signaled for Irene to accompany her down the aisle. By the time they were halfway to the stage, quiet had fallen over the theater. Together they pulled back the curtain that spanned the stage. Then they found two empty seats and sat back to escape to another world.

Gavin watched his mother during supper. She looked as if she was about to collapse from fatigue. He knew that, along with a nagging cough, dealing with Wesley had her worn to a frazzle. Some peace and quiet would probably do her a world of good.

He raised his palms and slapped them together for attention. "I have an idea. I got paid today, and there's money burning a hole in my pocket. Would anyone like to go to the movies?"

Solemn faces transformed instantly into big grins. "Yes, yes," Jenny squealed, hopping up and down in the middle of the floor. Cassie tried to act more adult. She merely smiled and nodded.

"As soon as the kitchen is clean and wood brought in for the night, we'll go to town."

They jumped to their tasks and were ready to leave in record time.

"It's too cold for anyone to ride in back of the truck," Gavin decreed as they left the house. "You can all pile into the cab tonight."

They did. And the older ones didn't complain about having the younger ones sit on their laps—including Wes.

When he reached town, Gavin turned right at the main intersection and drove to the parking lot of the movie theater at the south end of town. The only place open besides the theater was the ice-cream parlor at the opposite end of Main Street.

"Do you have enough money for us to have some popcorn?" Lonnie asked as they filed into the theater lobby.

Gavin grinned. "I think so. But we need to hurry. It's time for the show to start."

The cartoon was playing as they trooped inside the already darkened theater with their popcorn. Gavin had even bought a package of gum for them to share later.

He found pleasure in treating the kids. Because of her circumstances, Mom had been forced to rely on them for work beyond what most kids had to do. Much as it had been for him, only for different reasons.

Until now Gavin had been content with his solitary life. But the delight he felt at making his younger siblings happy made him wonder what it would be like to have a family of his own.

They tiptoed down the aisle and filed into a row of seats that had a half dozen empty ones. Quietly they focused on the animated film on the screen and munched their popcorn.

When the cartoon ended, there were a couple of minutes before the newsreel started. Suddenly Cassie pointed ahead of them. Excited, she leaned over and whispered into his ear. "That's Miss Delaney."

Gavin's emotions went haywire. It was ridiculous how the mere thought—or sight—of Irene made his heart beat faster. But the memory of their last encounter still rankled. His boss had not been happy when he had to put in a request for a refund to Mr. Delaney. And he didn't know how to react to Irene now. Did she blame him that she would not be getting electricity?

As if sensing his stare, she shifted in her seat and glanced back over her shoulder. He saw her go still and then quickly turn around. Yes, she had recognized them. He knew it.

He tried to focus on the screen. But he couldn't keep his eyes from gravitating back to Irene. She and the girl next to her leaned close to one another and whispered. He sensed that Irene had told her friend who was behind them.

A kernel of popcorn flew through the air and landed in Irene's hair. She reached back and brushed it away, but she didn't turn around.

Gavin leaned forward and aimed a stern look at Wes. He mouthed the words *Do you want to go home?*

The other kids glared at their troublemaking brother.

Wes shook his head, folded his arms across his chest and stared straight ahead. Anger radiated from him. Well, too bad. His behavior had gotten tiresome.

When the double-feature movies ended and the lights came on, Gavin stretched his muscles. He hadn't cared much for the swashbuckler, but he had liked the Tom Mix Western.

The kids didn't seem in a hurry to leave, so they remained in their seats while people exited past them. When their teacher and her friend came even with their row, Jenny raised a hand. "Hi, Miss Delaney."

Irene and her friend stopped and let people go on past them. "Why, hello, Jenny. And Cassie. Lonnie. Wesley. And Gavin." She looked from one to the other of them. "It looks like you've had a nice evening out."

Gavin wasn't sure he liked being greeted in such a nonpersonal way, just lumped in with the kids. But he understood that she would not welcome one-on-one conversation with him.

"Hello," her friend said. "I'm Rayona Mitchell." She reached a hand toward Gavin. "Irene told me that you're the older brother of these four." Her expression and tone were just a tad flirtatious.

"We would love to visit," Irene said. "But Rayona has to work, and I'm helping her."

Jenny tipped her head to one side. "What kind of work?"

She hesitated a moment but then explained. "We ushered and helped in the concessions before the movie. Now we have to sweep the floors and clean the restrooms."

"We'll help you." Jenny looked over at Gavin. "We can, can't we?"

Gavin looked at Miss Mitchell, certain she didn't want them hanging around. But she surprised him.

"Well, there are two jobs that need to be done," she said, glancing around the now lit and nearly empty room. "We have to check the seats and scrape off all the gum we find."

Gavin saw Wes duck his head and knew there would be a wad under the seat where he had sat.

"What's the other job?" Jenny wanted to know.

"Well, there's always leftover popcorn," Rayona said, adopting an air of innocence. "And someone has to eat it."

Both girls squealed. "We can do it. Can't we, Gavin?" They turned imploring looks on him.

He grinned and shook his head in resignation. "Get busy."

"Come with me." Rayona led them into the lobby and over to the concession stand, where a man and woman had just gone behind the counter.

"Mom. Dad. I have helpers this evening. How much popcorn do we need to get rid of?"

Mr. Mitchell looked over the little group. "About a half gallon." His dark eyes sparkled behind black-framed glasses.

"We use these paint scrapers." Rayona went behind the counter and reached below it. She handed one to each kid. "As soon as you're done, wash your hands and come back here."

They scurried away.

"What can I do?" Gavin asked.

John Mitchell shrugged and waved off the idea. "Just stay and visit with us. We're always glad to have Irene around, and her friends are welcome."

Irene didn't seem all that pleased about it, though. Gavin could feel the cool barrier she had erected between them. He spoke to Mr. Mitchell but visually followed Irene's movements as she scooped the last of the popcorn from the machine. "How is business doing?"

"Oh, fair to middlin'. We change movies three times a week, but the weekends still draw the best crowds. We run some special promotions at the matinees. As a matter of fact, we've just worked out an arrangement with Miss Delaney. Any of her students who score a hundred in spelling for six weeks straight wins a free ticket to the Saturday matinee."

Gavin looked over at Irene. She gave him a tiny smile that sent a tide of warmth through him. "You planning to make champion spellers of them?"

"That's the idea." She made one final scoop and dumped it in the big bowl that was nearly full.

For several minutes the Mitchells chatted about their business and current happenings in the small town. Gavin enjoyed the visit, but he felt tongue-tied in Irene's presence. He wanted to talk to her, get to know her better, maybe fall in love with her. But he couldn't forget that last scene at her home. It worried him that she captivated him, and he was afraid to pursue her. She had dreams—and an intimidating father.

Yet, in spite of that, he edged his way down the counter until he could speak directly to her. He would ask her to go for a drive with him Sunday afternoon. Rejection would be a tough blow. But he had to take a chance.

Their eyes held for a timeless moment. Struggling to control his emotions, he opened his mouth. "I—"

Suddenly, without warning, the entire theater went dark.

Chapter 6

"He only pushed a switch," Irene muttered as she drove home, her anger not yet cooled. Was nothing safe around the boy?

Pity for Gavin seeped through her. He had been frustrated and obviously embarrassed at having to demand yet another apology from his little brother. When Gavin refused to let them stay to eat the leftover popcorn there in the lobby, Mrs. Mitchell had put it in a sack and given it to Cassie to take home with them.

Irene didn't sleep well that night, unable to stop the troubled cycle of her thoughts. As she labored to get the washing done Saturday morning, she wished Jolene had not invited her and Dad to supper tonight. But the invitation had been issued and accepted before the atmosphere at home had become so strained. Knowing Jolene, she would already have pies baked and plans made. They couldn't back out now, even if there was so much work to do.

Irene thought longingly of Mrs. Mitchell's electric washing machine. *Lord, help me not be envious.*

That afternoon Irene picked up the bowl of potatoes she'd told Jolene she would bring and headed for the car. She detoured by the smokehouse, where she saw the door open and peeked inside. Her dad was moving meat around to take up less space.

"I'm going on over to Jolene's."

Without stopping what he was doing, he barely glanced at her. "I'll ride Diamond over in time to eat."

Anxious to escape the house and spend some time with her sister's baby, Irene left immediately. Already three months old, little Rolen Blake was the joy of Jolene's and Riley's lives. They had begun to despair of having a family when they learned Rolen was on the way after nearly three years of marriage. Irene was thrilled for them and loved her young nephew. She knew it would be hard for Jolene to return to school this fall, but her sister felt that since God had given her the gift of teaching, she had a responsibility to use it.

Riley had run the gas station in town for a year after they first married. But then Dave Freeman, the owner, had returned from the city, where he had been while his wife underwent extensive medical treatment. Dave now ran his station again, and Riley had gone back to working at the sawmill with his dad. Business had been better recently, and Riley had proven to be a good farmer. They had a few cattle and some chickens, and they raised a huge garden.

"If you'll put Rolen down long enough, we'll eat," Jolene announced a few minutes after Sam arrived.

They took their places at the kitchen table, and Riley blessed the food. Tall and good-looking, he possessed the muscles of a hardworking man. After years of rejecting

God because of anger over his brother's tragic death as a teenager, Riley had gotten past his anger and become a committed Christian. He and Jolene attended the Deer Creek Mission together.

Irene took a piece from the platter of fresh bread and passed it to her left.

Sam forked a slice of ham and passed that platter. "I know I had another ham in the smokehouse," he muttered with a shake of his head, staring at the food on his plate.

"I guess we're both losing track of things," Riley said. "I know I had another bag of cow feed in the feed house."

"Maybe you're both losing your memory," Jolene suggested in a joking manner.

"I don't think so." Riley took the gravy bowl from her and spooned some over his bread.

"I aim to keep my eyes open for varmints," Sam added.

Irene didn't like the sound of this. She would take a look in the smokehouse for herself when she got home.

"I sure hope we can avoid getting drawn into that war situation overseas," Jolene commented during a break in the conversation.

"The U.S. already has over three hundred fifty thousand troops in the military." Riley's tone oozed concern. "I've been reading and listening to everything I can since Germany invaded Poland four months ago. The Germans invaded six countries and took them over within a three-month period. I'm afraid we'll have no choice but to get involved at some point."

A thread of fear trickled through Irene. She shared his concerns. She got up and went to get the chocolate cake and bring it to the table. She went back for the bowl of peaches as Jolene served the cake.

Jolene changed the subject. "We would give the REA

the easement they need through here. But the men we talked to said our location is not good. They said that if they don't find another property owner to sign up within this mile of road, we may not get a line."

Irene knew Jolene wanted electricity as much as she did. "Do you know if Juanita Tomlin has signed up?"

Sam clunked his fork down on the table. "That's enough!" He shoved his chair back and stalked from the room. A minute later the front door slammed.

They all sat in stunned silence. Irene stared at the cake left on Dad's plate. Then she blew a long breath of air through her pursed lips. "I'm not sure I have the nerve to go home."

The baby put up a howl from the other room. Jolene got up and went to get him.

"Stay a little longer," Riley advised Irene. "Give Sam some time to cool off."

She washed the dishes and left when Jolene came to dry them. "I'll see you at church in the morning," she said as she put on her coat. "Thanks for the meal."

When she got home, Irene tiptoed into the living room, not wanting to encounter her dad. He had been so moody and short-tempered lately that she wasn't sure what to expect. But he had already gone to his room. She stood outside the closed door and heard him snoring.

Relieved, she lit an extra lamp and ironed the basket of clothes she had dampened before going to Jolene's. It was late when she finished and crawled into bed.

Sunday morning she woke early and fixed breakfast. When Dad came to the table, he seemed subdued but made no mention of the evening before. He was quiet but agreeable during the ride to and from church.

After dinner he put on his hat and coat and left the house. Irene peeked out the window and saw him walk with purpose past the barn and head across the pasture. She knew from following him as a girl that there was a big rock down behind the pond where he went to pour out his heart to God when he was troubled.

An hour later he returned and went to his room. His eyes were red rimmed.

"Why don't you go to church with us again?" Jenny's freckled face peered up at Gavin.

"I have work I need to do."

"You're not supposed to work on Sunday."

He reached out and swiped at her chin. "Do you always wear your breakfast on your chin?"

She wrinkled her nose. "You're not listening to me."

"No, I'm not," he agreed, and headed for the door.

He did have work that needed to be done, but he didn't want to do it. Nor did he want to be around people. And if he let Jenny talk him into going to church, he would see the people he did not want to see.

Ignoring his truck, he hiked to the barn behind the house and kept going. The frigid air hurt his lungs and froze his nose, so he walked faster to help keep warm.

Irene Delaney's soft mouth and dark gaze swam behind his eyes. She was gutsy, hardworking and pretty. But they had nothing in common. She had an enduring faith in God that he lacked. And she intended to leave once the school year ended. But he thought she was not indifferent to him. He drew in a huge gulp of the cold air—and nearly strangled on it.

Her dad obviously couldn't stand him.

Suddenly he drew up short. Running from his problems would not solve them. And he couldn't leave his mother to wrestle the wagon and team in this cold. His truck was at the house, but she did not drive.

He turned and nearly ran back to the house. He caught her at the barn rounding up the horses. "Get the kids. I'll take you to church."

She gave him an odd look but pulled the bridle from the mare and released her. "Did you change your mind about going?"

He shook his head. "No, but I need to run some errands and can take you to church on my way out. I'll come back and get you," he added before she could ask how they would get home.

"Thanks," she murmured, and headed for the house.

After Gavin dropped his family at the church, he drove to town, circled the empty streets and drove back to the school. He parked and sat in the truck with his thoughts until it was time to return to the church. Now what?

Back at the house, still restless, he didn't turn off the engine as Mom and the kids got out of the truck. "I don't know what time I'll be home."

Mom looked back at him in surprise. "You're not coming in to eat?"

"No. See you later."

After a brief hesitation, she shut the door and followed the kids into the house.

On impulse Gavin drove back to town and continued about a mile on the other side of it. He pulled in at the home of his old friend Dale Monroe. Before he got to the door, it opened.

"Hey, Gav. It's about time you showed up." Dale extended a hand across the threshold. "Get in here before we freeze."

"I've been busy." He stepped through the doorway. The warmth felt wonderful. The scent of cinnamon and onions filled the air.

"You look tired. I heard you were back and working for the REA."

Gavin removed his hat. "It's a good job, but it's more than that. It's a cause."

Dale's grin revealed a gap between his front teeth. "I agree. It's not right for rural people to live as second-class citizens. It must be tough for you to come back to the country after living in the city, though. Say, have you eaten?"

Gavin waved off the question. "I'll get something later."

"We're just sitting down to dinner. Join us."

"Please." Carolyn Monroe's voice came from the kitchen door.

Gavin turned to stare at her. Tall and blonde, Carolyn Ellis had been his first girlfriend. When he was thirteen—Wes's age—he had become aware of girls as more than plagues to be endured. Carolyn had been the one who captured his attention, and she had returned the interest. But the summer between grade school in the country and starting high school in town, her interest had transferred to his buddy Dale. Gavin had also become interested in someone else. But he and Carolyn had remained friends throughout school. He had even been best man at her wedding to Dale.

"I didn't come looking for a handout."

Her cheeks dimpled. "Then eat while you tell us what you *did* come for."

"The truth is I didn't come for anything," he admitted, raking a hand over the back of his neck. "I just needed to get away from the house for a while."

"Ah, you need a sympathetic ear. Girl trouble?"

Gavin jerked his head back and forth rapidly.

"You're not seeing anyone?"

"No."

Dale's mouth crinkled at the corners. "Anyone you'd like to see?"

A telling pause gave him away.

"So that's the problem. Come to the table and tell me about it."

Gavin followed Dale to the kitchen and sat where Carolyn had just added another plate. "Not everyone is willing to do what's necessary to get a power line through here."

"Who in particular?" Dale placed a napkin in his lap and handed Gavin the bowl of potatoes.

After dipping a helping, Gavin drew a deep breath and explained about the easements. But he didn't name Sam.

Dale's head bobbed in understanding. His eyes rolled up in thought. "I'm remembering that stretch of road through your neck of the woods. Which family has a daughter the right age to catch your interest and tie you in knots? Parker? No. Davis? No. Lonigan? No." He ticked them off on his fingers. Then he snapped them. "Delaney. Sam's youngest daughter is the teacher out there now. She has to be the one."

Gavin drew in a long, slow breath. "He's a good man. He just doesn't see how much difference electricity would make in their lives, especially for the women. And asking for an easement made him explode."

"Doesn't sound like the Sam Delaney I know." Dale put his fork down and extended his left hand to Gavin. He clasped his wife's with his right. "Let's pray about this."

Without hesitation he bowed his head. "Lord, we ask Your guidance in this matter. Please remove any bad feelings that everyone involved may have and open their hearts to whatever You would have them do. Amen."

Gavin didn't know if God was listening, but some of the weight lifted from his heart.

Irene rode an emotional merry-go-round all day Monday. She no longer knew what to expect from her normally mild-mannered dad. She heaved a sigh and gathered her papers from the desk.

Outside the school, she shivered as the stiff January wind whipped her hair into disarray. She pulled her coat closer around her and glanced across the road at the frozen pond on the Blake property. Though it was stark and pale now, come spring there would be frogs croaking and all kinds of life around it. The wind buffeted her as she got in the car. It took four tries to get the motor started.

She had barely gotten home and removed her coat when her dad came in the back door. He took off his gloves, blew on his hands and rubbed them together. "Looks like a storm building in the east. I brought in extra wood. Are you ready for me to build a fire in the cookstove for you?"

Irene struggled to grasp his mood. He seemed normal. But there was a stiffness in his shoulders and his manner seemed hurried.

The sound of an engine outside drew her attention. She peeked out the window. Oh, no, Gavin had returned. She couldn't bear to listen to any more unpleasantness. She backed toward the kitchen. "I'll build the fire. You get the door."

She pulled the ash box from the stove and took it out the back door to empty it. When she returned, she couldn't help but listen for sounds from the living room. A draft of cold air wafted clear into the kitchen when the door opened.

"Hello, Mr. Mathis. Come inside," she heard Dad greet Gavin.

She stepped to one side just enough to see him enter the living room, hat in hand. In the pewter-gray of dusk, he was an impressive figure. He wore sensible work boots and a chocolate-brown hat. Her breath grew shallow at the tentative smile on his face.

"Got your message, Sam. The office secretary said you want to talk to me."

Dad had been to see him? What was he up to? Irene had an urge to go run interference between them. But her feet remained rooted to the floor.

"I hope…"

"I want…"

They spoke simultaneously.

Sam stuck out a hand. "Young man, I owe you an apology. I took my personal frustrations out on you, and the Lord took me to task about it. He also reminded me of some things."

Gavin acknowledged his words with a shrug. "I probably didn't handle matters well."

"Have a seat and let's talk business."

When Gavin moved beyond her line of vision, Irene returned to the stove and began to stuff corncobs into the firebox. While she lit a fire, she listened in amazement as they discussed restoring their sign-up and granting of an easement.

"Thank you for being so understanding," her dad said when they finished. "I'm an old dog, so I learn slow. But I think I understand things better now. We've been through some real tough times these past few years, but we've hung on with everything we've got to stay on our land and make a living. We even found ways to invest in some new machines that make farmwork easier and faster. But our tractors and combines don't make the women's work easier. The Lord helped me see that electricity and indoor plumbing can do that for them. It's their turn."

"I'll get the paperwork drawn up tomorrow," Gavin promised.

"You're on a mission, and I wish you the best. If there's anything I can do to help you, let me know."

"Thank you, sir. I'll let you know if there is. Would it be all right if I speak to your daughter before I leave?"

Irene bent over the stove and relit the fire that had flickered out. The damper created only a small draft even on a breezy day like today, and the fire often flickered out multiple times before catching into full flames. She blew on the tiny embers, trying to coax it to life. Ashes whirled up in her face.

"Let me do that."

She stepped back and wiped her face as Gavin stuffed more corncobs into the firebox and tightened their arrangement. She edged closer to watch.

He relit the fire and moved back. Then he turned to face her. "I think it'll burn now."

"Thank you. Now, what can I do for you?"

A muscle in his cheek twitched. He scrubbed his jaw with one hand. "I just thought, since I'm here, I'd ask about Wesley's behavior. Is there any improvement?"

"Nothing earth-shattering has happened so far this week. I guess that could be called an improvement." She grinned.

"Of course, it's only Monday," he pointed out, his smile sending her heart into near cardiac failure.

He reached over and ran a finger over her chin. "Ashes. But you wear them nicely."

Irene automatically reached up, and their hands brushed.

She lowered her lashes to keep from revealing the inner turmoil his touch caused.

Flustered and needing to occupy herself, she moved closer to the stove and picked up the teakettle, meaning to move it to one side, out of the way. It slipped from her nerveless fingers.

Chapter 7

Gavin couldn't stop grinning. He had thought Irene returned the attraction he felt toward her. Now he *knew* she did. Seeing her flustered had been satisfying.

Her embarrassment at the water spilled on the floor made him chuckle. He had taken the mop from her and wiped the floor while she refilled the kettle. He drew in a deep breath, remembering the warm, womanly scent of her. His heart beat faster.

Dale's prayer came to mind. Was God responsible for Sam's change of heart?

Close on the tail of that thought came a return of common sense. Building dreams around Irene was foolish. She planned to leave Deer Lick. But he couldn't control his internal reaction to her. He steered the truck onto the road to the house.

The present came rushing back to him in the form of three children racing across the yard toward him, the girls in hot pursuit of Wesley. What had the boy done now?

"Gavin!" Jenny shouted as he braked the truck to a stop.

With a sigh of inevitability, he got out. "What's wrong?"

Jenny pointed at Wes, who had stopped in the lane behind them. "He broke the window of our bedroom. Now we'll freeze in there."

"It was an accident," he yelled back at them.

Gavin nearly choked on exasperation. "All right, everybody calm down and tell me what happened."

"He was throwing his old baseball over the roof of the house," Cassie explained angrily. "And he hit the window."

"It slipped," Wes yelled in defense.

"Let's go inside and talk to Mom." *God, I sure could use some help here.*

Mom met them at the door, drawn by the racket. Her eyes glistened with tears. "Wesley, I'm about ready to turn you over to the sheriff," she threatened in a voice filled with sheer frustration. "You better find a way to replace that window."

"I don't have any money," he protested.

"Then you better find a way to get some." She spun and went back inside the room.

Gavin followed the kids inside. "Let's get it boarded over for now."

Irene stared inside the smokehouse again, looking for evidence of varmints. She saw nothing that indicated something, or someone, had gotten in there and taken anything. Dad must have miscounted the hams.

As she returned to her tasks, she couldn't keep from recalling her clumsiness in Gavin's presence. She tried to explain to herself why she turned to soft butter around him.

"Leave me alone," she muttered. "I can't waste time daydreaming."

The next day was a typical school day with no major behavior problems. After reading and spelling lessons, they took a morning recess. Arithmetic followed, and then they had lunch. After some outdoor play time, they studied geography, language and civics. Irene stood at the door as the students filed out of the building at four o'clock. Zada and Wesley remained behind.

To her surprise, an old car pulled into the schoolyard. Her middle-aged, slightly balding pastor got out and came to the door, his expression impossible to read.

"Hello, Brother Jacob," she greeted him. "Come inside where it's warmer."

He peered past her into the building. When he saw the two students still present, he smiled and followed her. She shut the door and faced him. "How may I help you?"

He smiled as if uncertain. "I don't know if you know this, but my wife's brother is a singing master who travels around the country conducting singing schools."

Irene nodded. "I remember it being mentioned."

He cleared his throat. "Well, Reginald is coming for a long visit, and he has agreed to do a school for us while he's here."

She frowned. "Those schools are usually held in the summer."

He nodded. "Right. But I think we can get a good turnout for one. He'll be here week after next, so I have time to make a lot of contacts."

Irene doubted he would have to make too many. The two-week schools often resembled tent revivals. They were a large social event for a small town. Nearly everyone able to do so would attend, and others would come from miles around. Hosting such a school would be a huge accomplishment for Brother Jacob.

"There's one problem, though," he continued. "His wife usually travels with him and plays the piano for the schools, which works fine in the summers. But right now they have two kids in school, and she feels she needs to stay home with them. I told him we have a very accomplished accompanist in our membership. Will you do it?"

Irene drew a deep breath, considering what her commitment would mean.

"I know you have a long schedule here at school, with housework waiting for you when you get home," he went on hurriedly, obviously fearing a refusal. "Would it help if some of the members helped with your laundry and meals?"

"Jolene will be happy to feed Dad and me," Irene said slowly. "The housework can slide, and I can use Saturdays to catch up and do the laundry."

Sensing her agreement, he visibly relaxed. "Thank you, Irene. You're such a blessing to our church and community. I know the Lord will bless you."

"It starts a week from Monday night?"

"Yes. I'll call Reginald and tell him to plan on teaching."

Excitement bubbled in Irene when she got home from school to find two electrical workers at the farm. With a tape, they measured off spacing for electric poles. Then they painted symbols on stakes and drove them into the ground. When they finished, they moved on down the line away from the house.

She sighed in satisfaction and started to go into the house. But she paused on the porch when she spied a truck coming down the road. It got almost past the drive-

way, stopped and backed up. Gavin Mathis got out. His
mouth curved upward at the corners as he crossed the
yard toward the porch.

"I just thought I'd stop and say hello, since I saw you
out here," he said cheerfully. He looked good in dark
pants and a navy blue coat. "I'm on my way home to eat
with Mom and the kids. Then I have to get to another
meeting."

"Still selling people on electricity?"

He shrugged and took off his hat. "Most people don't
require much selling. But they have lots of questions
about all that's involved in creating the power network."

"And you're the guy with all the answers, huh?" She
hugged her school papers and book to her chest.

"I wouldn't say that, but after answering the same
questions over and over, I can usually satisfy people's
curiosity."

She tipped her head to one side. "Test time. We've
been told for years now that it was too expensive to build
power lines in sparsely populated areas. What changed?"

"Three things drove down the cost," he said without
hesitation. "One is the use of high-strength conductors
that permit longer spans, reducing the number of poles
per mile from about thirty to eighteen. Second is the de-
velopment of a single-phase line with light and tough
poles minus the cross-arms. And the third is putting con-
struction on an assembly-line basis in place of the old
pole-by-pole methods."

He paused and grinned at her. "Does that answer pass
your test?"

"Excellent, thank you."

"Now it's your turn to answer questions."

"Ask away."

"Mom and the girls are talking about a singing school

and want me to take them. Is it worth the time and effort?"

"Of course. Learning music theory, sight-reading, conducting and harmony provides our churches with a supply of competent singers and persons capable of leading
congregational singing. The community also benefits."
She gave him a teasing grin, but she really did want to
convince him of the worth of such a school. "Many young
men and women consider these schools important to their
courtships. It's not unusual for the entire life of a town
to be put on hold so everyone can come."

Amusement glinted in his dark eyes. "So you think
they'll love it and learn a lot."

"No question about it," she assured him.

He gnawed at his lower lip. "I don't see how I can
manage the time every night for two weeks. I have meet-
ings scheduled."

She considered his plight. "Have the kids tell me at
school if there's a night you can't come. I'll pick them
up."

"Does that mean you're involved?"

"Of course. Do I pass?"

He hesitated, a blank look on his face for a moment.
Then he beamed a lightbulb smile at her. "You pass with
flying colors." He replaced his hat. "Well, I need to get
moving."

"One more thing," Irene said before he took more than
two steps. "If you bring them any night and need to leave
for a meeting, I'll bring them home."

"Thanks."

She watched him stride back to his truck and felt her
heart go with him. She shook her head at herself. *Stop
thinking of him as an attractive man. He's just the field
man who's working to carry out his company's objec-*

tives. And even if that weren't the case, it's a waste of time to get fanciful about a relationship with a man who doesn't share my faith.

The days sped by, with Wesley acting somewhat calmer. Irene didn't know what Nell Bozeman had said or done, but she thanked God for the results.

Monday night Dad started his chores a little early so he could go with her. At his usual insistence, Irene drove. She was glad he had decided to attend.

She steered past a big black dog that lay stretched in the churchyard and parked the car alongside the other cars and trucks. There were also some wagons, the teams staked out behind the cemetery on the south side of the church.

"Looks like you got a good turnout." Sam opened the door.

Irene smiled and scanned the crowd as they entered the church. Her heart gladdened when she spotted Gavin and his family seated near Jolene and Riley.

"I'll go sit with them." Sam spoke quietly and jerked his head toward their pew. "You go on and do whatever you need to do."

Pastor Jacob came toward her, a man following him, as Irene walked down the aisle to the front. His face beamed. "Hello, Miss Delaney. I'd like you to meet my brother-in-law, Reginald Paxson. He's a graduate of the Stamps-Baxter music school. Reggie, this is Irene Delaney, the gifted pianist I've been telling you about."

A giant of a man with a bulbous nose, Reginald Paxson extended a hand. "Thank you for helping us." His voice boomed and bounced off the walls. He handed her a book. "Jacob here assured me that you can play anything I put before you. We'll be using this edition of the

Stamps-Baxter songbook. I understand you've been playing for the church since you were quite young."

She nodded. "The members were always supportive and encouraged me to come to the church and practice on their piano before I had one of my own. I owe them a lot."

"She's a treasure, not only to our church but to the entire community," the pastor bragged.

Uncomfortable at the praise, Irene glanced up at the clock on the wall. "I'll help you in any way I can, Mr. Paxson."

"Please call me Reginald." The man's friendly words seemed at odds with his grizzly-bear size and voice.

Irene took her place at the piano when it was time to begin. Throughout the evening she sneaked glances at Gavin when she wasn't playing. At the end of two hours of lessons and exercises centered on pitch and harmonies, she debated whether to go speak to him. But she didn't get a chance.

Mr. Paxson detained her to outline his plans for the remaining nights of the school. By the time he finished, the Bozeman family and Gavin had left.

The next two nights followed a similar pattern. Thursday morning Cassie Bozeman approached Irene on the porch steps before classes began. "Gavin has a meeting tonight. He said he'll bring us to singing school, but he'll have to leave and would appreciate it if you will take us home."

She gave the young girl a warm smile. "I'll be happy to do that."

Irene delivered the Bozeman family to their home that night and enjoyed the brief time with Nell. Friday night Gavin was back in attendance with them. But he was not in church on Sunday.

Mixed feelings churned inside her as Irene prepared to

leave the house Monday night to begin the second week of singing school. Her dad had informed her he couldn't go that night, because he expected Bossy, his favorite jersey cow, to drop her calf at any time. They had eaten leftovers from Sunday's dinner rather than go to Jolene's to eat as they had done the week before.

Irene got in the car and tried to start the engine. When it barely chugged, sputtered and died, she tried again and got nothing. Frustrated, she smacked the steering wheel with her gloved hand. "I'll be late if I ride my bike." But she had no choice.

She got out and hurried to get it. She pedaled furiously and was rounding the corner at the end of their pasture when she heard a vehicle approaching behind her.

Gavin slowed the truck when he spotted a form on a bicycle in the road ahead of them, a long coat trailing behind the seat.

"That's Miss Delaney." Cassie's voice held excitement at recognizing her teacher.

Gavin rolled to a stop alongside where Irene had pulled to the side of the road for them to pass. Mom rolled down her window.

"Got car trouble?" he asked across the seat.

She nodded, her body visibly shaking from the cold. "Y-y-yes."

He put the truck in neutral and got out. "It's too cold for you to be out here in the dark riding that. Get in the truck. The kids can ride in the back."

Mom and the kids piled out. Mom held the quilt they kept in the truck. "You kids get up behind the cab and hunker down and put this over you."

"I c-can't take th-their seat," Irene protested.

"Yes, you can." His mom spoke firmly and put an arm around Irene's shoulders.

Thankful for her help, Gavin took the handlebars of the bike from Irene's hands. "I'll put this in the back. Snuggle up next to Mom and get warm."

Mom steered her to the open truck door. "You're smaller, so you get in the middle. Don't argue," she added when Irene started to balk. "This will also keep you from being late to the church."

He chuckled inwardly when Irene didn't argue the point. She got in and slid over to the center of the seat.

"The kids and bike are tucked in," he said as he got behind the wheel, aware that Irene was trying to keep some distance between them. He almost chuckled aloud when her arm touched his. Silently, and under cover of near darkness, he reached over and gave her hand a quick pat of assurance. And wished he could put his arms around her.

In the service that night he didn't understand the singing master's words about elements of echoes and alternating melodies, but he rejoiced in the turn of events that had provided the opportunity to be near Irene. He couldn't keep from watching her rather than paying attention to the singing instruction.

His mother tapped him on the arm and leaned over to flip the page of his songbook. "That's the wrong page," she whispered.

He forced his mind back to the lesson.

When he pulled up at Irene's house later that night, he resisted the urge to touch her before she slid across the seat after his mother got out to make way for her to exit. "I'll pick you up the rest of the week," he said before she could get away.

"Oh, you don't need to do that."

"We want to," his mother insisted. He could have kissed her.

"Well…tomorrow night," she agreed. "Maybe by Wednesday night Dad will have the car fixed. Thanks for the ride tonight."

"You're welcome. See you tomorrow night."

Irene waved at all of them and headed to the porch, her black hair bouncing against her neck. He waited until she disappeared inside the house before he put the truck back in motion.

"She's a sweet girl."

He couldn't see Mom's eyes, but her voice held meaning.

"She is. With a great future ahead of her."

"You don't sound exactly thrilled about that."

He sucked in a deep breath. "She'll leave this place behind, probably become famous."

"I doubt it. Her roots are here. And I've seen the looks passing between the two of you. You need a good woman in your life."

His spine stiffened. "She has her sights set on other things, other places. She told me she wants a career in music. She isn't interested in marrying and having a family. She deserves the chance to try her wings."

"I suppose so." She paused. "But I have a strong feeling she'll find God's plan for her isn't what she thinks it is."

Gavin pulled in at the house, thankful to end the subject.

The next night, he arrived home to be told by Cassie that Miss Delaney would ride to the church with her sister. He was disappointed, but it made it easier for him to go to a meeting he couldn't miss and return in time to pick up his family.

Friday night the church members served refreshments after the final lesson. He was relieved at the lightening of his schedule but sorry that he would no longer see Irene every night.

He went through the line with Mom and got a piece of cake and a cup of coffee. They found empty chairs across from one another at a table.

Mom put her plate down and looked over at him. "I haven't had a chance to talk to you."

Gavin examined her face but couldn't read her expression.

"Wes figured out a way to replace the window glass."

"How?"

She shifted in the chair, not answering until she had gotten settled. "He arranged a trade with Mr. Dooley at the hardware store. He promised to kill and deliver a dozen rabbits in exchange for the glass." Now she smiled. "Don't you think that's good?"

He nodded. "I do. You were right to make him replace it. He needed the lesson."

"I hope he learned from it." Her tone was wishful.

A burst of pleasure filled him when Irene appeared at their table. "Do you mind some company?"

"Glad to have you." He pulled out the chair next to him.

She set her plate and cup on the table and sat, smoothing the skirt of her navy blue dress over her legs. "Dave Freeman came out and fixed the car. It's long overdue for an overhaul and some other expensive repairs, but he did enough to get it going. I drove it tonight."

Happy to have her beside him, Gavin enjoyed the next few minutes of conversation.

Suddenly aware of how much quieter the room had grown, he looked over to where Wes and the girls had joined the Lonigan girls and some more friends earlier. The tables were empty. He gave Irene an uneasy look.

"I think I should check on the kids, make sure they're not up to anything they shouldn't be doing." Meaning Wes.

She pushed her chair back. "I'll go with you."

He looked over at his mom, who had started to get up. "Stay here and finish your pie, Mom. We'll be back in a few minutes."

She glanced from him to Irene and back and then eased back into her chair. "If Wes is up to trouble, bring him to me."

They left the room and headed down the hallway, peeking into each room they passed. Empty. His feelings of unease escalated.

"Wesley. Cassie," he called.

"In here." It was Cassie's voice.

They turned toward the sound and hurried into the auditorium. The young people had gathered in the choir seats to visit. All but Wesley. He was perched on the piano stool, making it spin around and around as fast as he could. As it spun, it rose higher and higher. Suddenly both the stool and the boy went tumbling to the floor.

The sight made Gavin go still. His first reaction was anger. Then, in a burst of insight, he realized that ranting, reasoning and punishing were not reaching Wesley. What his young brother needed was the companionship of an older man. Since Wes had no dad, Gavin needed to be that man. Which would mean spending less time with Irene. But why should that matter? He blocked the thought from his mind.

Chapter 8

As the days passed, men unloaded trucks of poles where the earlier crews had left the marked stakes. It made Irene almost giddy with anticipation every time she looked out the window or went outside and saw them. Her school days and housework, plus piano lessons in the evenings and on Saturday afternoons, kept her near exhaustion. She no longer had time to spend playing and singing after supper, as had been her habit for years. Bright rays of unseasonably warm sunshine for late February beamed through the windows, a welcome sight after so much frigid weather and snow.

The school building looked deserted when Irene arrived Monday morning. Zada was late. Irene paused in front of the door and stared down the road, looking for the girl. The two-acre plot on which the school sat was a couple hundred yards back from the gravel road and faced the Blake home almost directly across the road. The only indication of life over there was audible rather than visible, the sound of Riley and his dad running the saw at the mill. Hurriedly she took her belongings inside and began to build the fire Zada should already have started. She had just placed a pile of kindling in the stove when the girl came rushing through the door.

"I'm sorry, Miss Delaney. Daddy got a new job, and Mama is sick. I had to fix breakfast since she couldn't."

"I understand. It's okay." She did. Zada's family didn't function very well at their best. With her mother sick, and her older sister, Zona, spending some time with a relative in another town, Zada would be expected to take over. But Irene was glad to hear that Mr. Lonigan had a job. She wondered if it would last longer than any of the others he had gotten.

She arranged a couple of small pieces of wood over the kindling and lit it. "Why don't you fill the water bucket. I'll finish this."

"Thank you, Miss Delaney." The girl whirled and dashed to the table beside the classroom door that held a basin and a water pail with a dipper that everyone used. A towel hung from a hook near it. When the students arrived, they would place their lunch pails beneath it and hang their wraps on the hooks on the wall.

Once the flames licked greedily through the kindling and the wood caught fire, Irene added some larger chunks of firewood. Satisfied that it would burn, she closed the door and went to her desk.

Students soon began to arrive. As she checked the roll, Irene's eyes locked on the empty desk where Selma Holman normally sat. Friday, Velma had been the one absent. The day before that it had been Thelma. Each day for the past two weeks, two of the girls had been present but one absent. It troubled her. She put the record book away and had everyone stand to recite the Pledge of Allegiance before they began their lessons.

Irene was writing spelling words on the blackboard, the chalk squeaking, when she had another thought about the Holman girls. They all three had scored 100 percent on their spelling the past four weeks. If they scored 100 percent this week and again next week, they would qualify for the free matinee a week from Saturday. But how would their absenteeism affect them?

She turned to face the class. "Pansy, please pronounce the first word." She pointed at the list of words for the third graders.

When the spelling lesson ended, they put their books away and got their lunch pails. As they ate, Irene considered her finances. This Friday would be payday. She needed new shoes but didn't see how she could afford them.

Since the weather had been so bad, some of her piano students had been irregular about attendance, which meant a loss of earnings. Also, she had received no payment for the last two items she had submitted to the *Grit* newspaper. Could she get by for another month with holes eating through the soles of her shoes? She sighed in resignation. She would have to stuff them with cardboard and hope her dad didn't notice. She was grown now. She needed to take care of herself.

Shortly before dismissal time, Irene was writing homework assignments on the blackboard when she became aware of the unusual quiet—no papers rustling, no fidgeting in desk seats, no giggling or whispering—and slowly turned around.

Gavin had entered the schoolroom and was easing the door closed. She put the chalk down and walked back to where he stood, her heart thumping in alarm. "Is something wrong?"

He removed his hat and spoke softly. "I was out making rounds and stopped at the Harris home. No one answered my knock, but Mr. Harris made it to the door as I was leaving."

His compelling gaze made Irene's breath come in uneven spurts. She wanted so badly to reach up and brush back the lock of sandy hair that had fallen over his forehead. "He's so crippled with arthritis that he can hardly get around."

Gavin nodded. "I could see that. Anyhow, he said that his wife is very sick, and he's worried about her. I remembered your relationship with the woman and thought you would want to know."

His thoughtfulness touched her. "Of course I do. Thank you for stopping by to tell me. The students leave in less than an hour. I'll hurry home and get a few things to take over there."

He nodded politely. "If you'll tell me what time you think you can be ready, I'll meet you at your house and take you. I should be off work at five."

She squelched the spurt of happiness that rushed through her. This was not a pleasure outing. But having him along might prove useful. The elderly couple could be in worse shape than she anticipated. "I'll be ready by five."

"I'll be there by ten after." He turned and went out the door.

Irene raced home after school and went straight to the root cellar for a quart of canned soup that she took into the house. Then she wrote a note to her dad and placed it on the table for him to find when he came in from chores.

She was ready and waiting on the porch when Gavin

arrived, her coat pulled around her even though it had warmed up a little. He took the soup and carried it to the truck for her.

Irene sat stiffly on the seat beside him. Neither of them talked as he drove.

"I'll do whatever you tell me," he said as he pulled up in front of the Harris house.

Irene nodded and got out. She knocked on the door and then pushed it open. "Bill, it's Irene Delaney," she called through the small opening.

"Come on in," a weak voice called back.

She glanced back at Gavin and then went on inside the house. Bill Harris sat huddled in a big rocker, his hands on the chair arms as if to prop him in position. His eyes were dull, his cheeks sunken hollows. A big man once, he had withered to a bony frame.

Irene squatted before him. "Have you had your medicine?"

He shook his head. "Too hard to get to it." His voice came out so raspy he was hard to understand.

Pearl normally took care of him. "I'll get it if you'll tell me where to find it."

He pointed to his right. "In the little chest over the wash basin."

"Is there anything I can do?" she heard Gavin ask as she went to get the medicine.

"We don't farm anymore, but Pearl keeps a few chickens."

"I'll go feed them."

"Feed's on the shelf at the back. It's in a bucket with a lid on it," Bill called as footsteps went to the door.

"I'll find it."

Irene returned to the room as the door closed behind Gavin. She handed Bill his pills and a glass of water and then waited while he swallowed the pills and drained the glass. "Where's Willie?"

Bill set the glass on the table beside him. "He took his wife and daughter on a trip to Texas. They're supposed to be home Friday."

Willie, their only son, lived in a neighboring town and did some occasional traveling related to his job, but this trip apparently had been more of a vacation. Irene would check on Pearl and Bill daily until Willie returned. He kept pretty close tabs on his parents and couldn't have known his mother would get sick.

"I'll check on Pearl now."

Bill just dipped his head.

She found Pearl sleeping, her face pale and still. Irene leaned over the bed and touched her elderly friend's brow. Pearl didn't seem feverish, but her shallow breathing didn't sound good. She coughed, and her eyes opened. Deep lines defined her face beneath thin gray hair.

Irene helped her sit up so she could cough without strangling. After Pearl got her breath, she sagged against Irene's hip.

"How long has it been since you've eaten?" Irene peered down into the woman's face.

"Couple of days." Like Bill, she was so hoarse Irene could hardly understand her.

"I brought you some soup. If I heat it, will you try to eat a little bit?" Hopefully getting some nourishment into her would revive her strength a bit.

Pearl's head barely moved, but she nodded.

Irene eased her back down onto the pillow. "I'll be right back."

She went to the familiar kitchen and warmed the soup. Then she poured some into a bowl and returned to Pearl.

She raised the woman up in the bed and placed the pillows behind her back.

"I'll take care of Bill," Gavin said from the doorway, assessing the situation.

Pearl picked up the spoon, but Irene took it when the woman's hand trembled so much that she almost dropped it. "Let me help you." She knew how independent the retired postmistress could be, but Pearl didn't object, an indication of how sick she had to be.

"I wish I had known sooner that you're sick," Irene said as she refilled the spoon, knowing that the flu could be deadly, especially for older people.

After Irene had gotten a few bites into Pearl, she settled her back onto the bed. When Pearl stretched out and closed her eyes, Irene covered her with a quilt and rejoined Gavin in the kitchen, where he had just finished feeding Bill. As he took Bill back to his chair, Irene heated some water and washed up the dishes they had used, plus the dirty ones sitting in the sink. Then they left.

The sun had disappeared, but the air was calm and gray. Quiet flurries of snow came from the east. Drifts from the last snowfall lined the ditches either side of the road. By now Irene had grown a little more comfortable around Gavin. She sat back in the seat and gazed out at the pure, cold beauty of winter. "How is your work coming along?" she asked, needing to make conversation.

He glanced over at her and then back at the road. "Pretty good. Some days are more productive than others. The line crews have a lot of unskilled workers taken from employment rolls, along with farmers who join us just to get the job done. With few proper tools and not a lot of method, erecting these lines can be disorganized and slow. We're trying to change that."

He pulled in at her house. Neither of them moved for

several moments. She could hear Gavin breathing in the near darkness. His hand came over and covered hers. "She'll be all right."

"I'm…sure she will," Irene said, her voice unsteady. "Thanks for going and helping. And for letting me know they're sick."

He shot her a quick smile and reached to turn off the engine. Irene grabbed the door handle and got out before he could do something gentlemanly like walk her to the door. As she pushed the door shut, the sight of his strong face through the window made her suddenly want to kiss him. She turned and hurried to the house before he could read her mind.

Sunday morning Gavin drew a deep breath as he and his mother followed the kids into the church, not sure why he had come.

He knew it made his mother happy for him to be in church. Being a churchgoing man might set the right example for Wesley and Lonnie. But what about himself and God? And was it hypocritical of him that knowing Irene would be here was a motivation to come?

Minutes later his foot moved in rhythm as her family group sang "I'll Fly Away." This was her world, her life.

The pastor took the pulpit and looked out at them in thoughtful contemplation for several moments before he began to speak. "According to the writer of Proverbs, conduct is the best indicator of character. All of us know, or have known, people who act one way in church but another way in their everyday lives."

Gavin's heart accelerated. He focused on the older man's words.

"A prime example of what I'm talking about is the Pharisees in the Bible. Jesus condemned them for professing godliness but denying that profession with sin in their lives. Appearances and words can be deceiving."

"God despises hypocrisy," the pastor continued. "Our task is to make sure our lives honor God. He deserves our total dedication. Love for others is what proves we are genuine children of God."

The words seemed to be aimed directly at Gavin. He glanced around at the people in the pews. No, they were not perfect. Many of them had major problems and flaws in their lives. But they came to worship together and helped one another. This past week a number of them had formed a team and taken turns looking in on Pearl and Bill Harris. They had delivered food to the couple and done chores for them, acts of genuine caring. They were good people, not hypocritical, as his stepfather had been.

"Let's don't be like the hypocrites. Let's model by words and actions what it means to follow the Lord. Let's love from a pure heart and sincere faith."

Gavin swallowed. It was time to stop looking at the behavior of others and be more concerned about his own behavior and motives.

Lord, give me guidance and strength.

After dinner he put on his hat and coat, feeling compelled to act on an idea that had been germinating in the back of his brain all week.

Mom looked up from her Bible reading. "You leaving?"

Gavin gave her a nod and a smile. "I want to check on something. I won't be gone long."

He got in his truck and drove to the Harris home. At the door, he knocked and then eased the door open to speak through the opening as Irene had done. "Mr. Harris, are you there? It's Gavin Mathis."

"We're here. Come in, young man."

When Gavin entered the room, he saw that Pearl lay on the sofa with a blanket over her.

He held his hat in his hands. "It's good to see you looking better, ma'am."

She smiled up at him. "It feels good to be out of bed, even if only to get this far."

"Do your chickens need to be fed?"

She nodded. "They could probably use a nibble."

"I'll be right back." He went to the chicken house and fed the twenty or so Rhode Island Reds. Then he stopped behind the building for another look at the old Ford car that sat abandoned there. Would it do for what he had in mind? He thought so.

He returned to the house and entered without knocking. "The biddies are happy now," he reported.

"Sit and chat a spell if you got time." Bill pointed at a chair.

Gavin sat and placed his hat on his knee. "There is something I'd like to ask you."

The old man's eyes squinted. "Ask away."

"What are you going to do with that old Ford sitting behind the chicken house?"

"Get rid of it if I can. You got any use for it?"

Gavin's spirits rose. "I might. How much do you want for it?"

Bill's face furrowed. "Well, let's see. It's a 1925 Model T Ford coupe that's seen its better days, but I think it'll run if you fix it up. I probably ought to pay you to haul it off. But I'd settle for a few more days of feeding Pearl's chickens."

A wide grin spread across Gavin's face. "I can do that. I didn't come prepared to haul it away, but I'll come back for it next weekend if that's okay with you."

"That'll be fine."

Gavin whistled all the way home.

Weary beyond words, Gavin got in his truck and headed home from work Tuesday afternoon. The weather remained cold, but it hadn't snowed and sleeted as much as in some winters he could remember. Even though it was almost March, Missouri weather could change at a moment's notice, so people tried to stay prepared for anything.

As he drove alongside the Delaney pasture, he could see their house on the other side of the field. Just as he started to round the corner, a flash of color caught his eye. He slowed to a stop and backed up to where he could get another look. Something colorful lay near a pole that had been unloaded where it would be erected.

He pulled to the side of the road and parked. It was probably nothing, but he would check anyhow. He hopped across the ditch, ducked between strands of the barbed-wire fence and set off across the field.

When he got near the pole, he saw that it was an item of clothing. A shirt? Why would workmen take off a shirt this time of year?

When he got closer, he realized that it was not a man's shirt but a woman's blouse—a very pretty woman's blouse. He picked it up and stared over at the Delaney house, where he could see a clothesline stretched across the backyard near the pasture fence. It must have blown off in Saturday's windstorm.

He picked it up and headed that way.

Irene slipped out the back door and crossed the yard to the swing Dad had hung from the huge oak tree years ago. She and Jolene had whiled away many an hour in it during their childhoods. Irene still came out here since Jolene had married and moved to her own house.

The old swing creaked as she settled into it and tucked her black coattail around her legs. She gripped the ropes and stared off into the distance. This was where she sought refuge when she needed to be alone to think.

She leaned back and moved her feet just enough to set the swing into gentle motion. Lost in her thoughts, she heard nothing around her. So she yelped when a pair of hands touched her shoulders.

She jerked her head around and found Gavin behind her. Mischief played across his handsome face, from the upturned corners of his mouth to his amused aquamarine eyes. His healthy male fragrance mingled pleasantly with the tang of the light breeze.

His hands pushed against her shoulders, making the swing go a little higher. She pumped her legs, delighting in the thrill of having him there, as well as the remembered joy of reaching for the sky.

"Higher," she ordered, laughter bubbling from her.

He pushed harder.

She leaned back and pointed her feet upward.

Suddenly the rope snapped.

Chapter 9

Irene's breath caught as she flew through the air and landed with an undignified thump on the ground. She tried to breathe—and couldn't.

Then Gavin was kneeling beside her. His arm slid behind her shoulders and tipped her forward. "Are you okay?"

Irene struggled for breath and managed to open her eyes. She stared at him for what seemed endless moments before she managed to draw a gulp of air and tried to answer. When she failed to form words, she waved a palm and forced a slight nod of her head. "I'm…'kay," she finally croaked.

He eased her to a sitting position and released an audible breath of relief. "I'm sorry I—"

She pressed a hand to his. "Not…your fault. I was…having fun," she finished in a rush. The cold air enveloped them, but neither moved.

"Why are you here?" she finally asked, self-conscious

at being this close to him. She could still hardly breathe or speak, but it was no longer from the tumble.

"I found that—" he pointed behind them "—in the field and brought it to you."

Irene spotted her missing blue blouse hanging across the clothesline and smiled. "I thought I had lost it. Thank you."

Light danced in the deep pools of his eyes when she looked back at him. He gave her hand a light squeeze. "I'm glad I found it."

Irene knew she should get up, but her body and brain refused to obey her common sense. She remained motionless, her gaze fused to his.

Gavin nudged her chin up, bringing their faces to within mere inches of one another, so close that his warm breath brushed her lips.

"You look okay…better than okay." His soft voice made her insides quiver. Her chest rose and fell in an erratic rhythm, but she could not look away. She moistened her lips with the tip of her tongue.

He brushed his knuckles against her cheek, his gaze focused on her mouth.

As a rush of dizzy pleasure overcame her, Irene reached up and stroked the hair that lined his forehead. Her fingers trailed to his temple—and froze at the sound of a car coming up the road. It pulled in at the house.

Irene scrambled to her feet, relieved at the interruption but disappointed at not experiencing what Gavin's kiss would be like.

She crossed the backyard and rounded the corner of the house. When she recognized the car, she looked back at Gavin. "It's the marshal."

He retrieved her blouse from the clothesline and brought it to her. "Should I leave?"

She shook her head. "Whatever he has to say might be of interest to you."

Leon Gentry strode toward the porch, but then he spotted them coming around the house and came to a halt. "Hello, Irene. Gavin."

"What can I do for you?" Irene asked.

The marshal frowned. "Nothing directly. I'm just making the rounds, warning people to keep a close eye on their property. We've had several reports of petty thievery in the area."

His words sparked a memory. "What kind of things are being taken?"

"Chickens. Animal feed. Small supplies."

"Food?"

His brow furrowed. "You have something missing?"

"Well, Dad said we're short a ham in the smokehouse. And Riley—" she jerked her head in the direction of his and Jolene's house "—thought he had a bag of cow feed go missing."

"Sounds like someone is doing their shopping from the neighborhood stores." He emphasized the last word with an ironic twist of his mouth. "Put locks on any doors that don't have them."

With a wave of his hand, he turned and left.

"Hey, Leon," Gavin called after him.

The marshal paused and turned.

"How about a ride to my truck. I left it the other side of the field."

"Get in."

Gavin turned to face Irene. "I'll see you around." Then he loped after Leon.

Irene stood there watching them all the way to Gavin's truck before going to pick up the remains of her broken swing.

* * *

"Hey, Wes, want to help me with something after we finish chores?" Gavin asked as they headed to the house with the milk buckets Saturday morning.

Wesley gave him a skeptical look. "Like what? More work?"

"I have to go get something I bought."

He grinned at his young stepbrother. Wes loved riding in the truck. "Yep, it's work. But there might be a driving lesson involved." *Sort of.*

The boy's eyes took on a glow, and a grin spread across his face. "Sure. When?"

"As soon as we finish chores, eat breakfast and round up some tow chains."

Their work speed picked up considerably.

When Gavin pulled in at the Harris home an hour later, Wes studied the property. When Gavin drove around behind the chicken house and backed up to the old car, the boy could not sit still. He craned his neck to peer out the window. "Are you taking that old junker home?"

Gavin nodded and stopped the truck. He looked over at Wes. "Do you think you and I could build a doodlebug?"

Wes shrieked and pumped a fist. "We sure can."

Irene arrived at the school several minutes before the 100 percent spellers of the past six weeks were to meet her there. Her heart sank when the Holman girls came walking into the schoolyard—the two Holman girls, seven- and eight-year-old Velma and Selma. Nine-year-old Thelma was not with them.

Irene waved them to the car. "Where's Thelma?" she asked as they got into the backseat.

There was a slight hesitation before Velma said in a small, shy voice, "She had to help Mama."

Irene sensed there was more to it than that, but the girls seemed unwilling to elaborate. Had they been told to not talk about their family troubles?

"Do you think she could go next Saturday, just her and me?"

The girls exchanged glances. Then their heads bobbed in unison. Their conversation ended with the arrival of the rest of their little group. Two of them sat in the front seat with Irene. The other six squeezed into the backseat, the three smaller ones sitting on the laps of the bigger ones. It was jam-packed, but they seemed to find it fun.

"We're going to the movies. We're going to the movies," Irene sang in a singsong fashion. They all joined in, laughing merrily.

Over the next week Irene's heart sank as the absenteeism of the Holman girls worsened rather than improved. Two of them were now absent every day. When questioned, the one present always gave a vague explanation about Mama needing them at home.

Life away from school was different. Her heart sang as she rushed home each day to meet her piano students, who were more regular now that the weather had improved. Everything she made from those lessons, as well as the payments that had finally arrived for the two articles to the *Grit* newspaper, went into her savings toward getting the house wired.

A hint of spring would bring freshness to the air one day, and then the next day they would be greeted with a soft layer of snow that melted before the day was over. It made Irene long to be outdoors. Sam hitched his horse, Diamond, to the plow every day and worked long hours turning the earth in preparation for planting.

The assembly trucks arrived that week. In accordance with the messages on the stakes in the ground, the crew unloaded insulation, nuts and bolts, a transformer, guy wires and anchors.

"It's really going to happen," she sang under her breath as she gazed at the mounds of supplies at each house on her way to pick up Thelma Saturday morning to attend the matinee. She had risen extra early to get the laundry washed and on the line to dry while she was gone, and she would be home in time for her afternoon piano lessons.

Thank you, God, for all You've done.

Gavin loved listening to Irene play the piano. He leaned back in the pew and let the melodies and extra little things she did at the keyboard flow through him. His thoughts churned as the music spoke to him.

He wished he had a better understanding of God. As a boy he had professed his belief in Him. Since then he had been through a wandering path of emotions and reactions toward his heavenly Father.

What more did he need to learn? What more did he need to do?

Read your Bible more. Get more involved in the church.

When the music had ended, he tried to keep his mind on the preacher's words, but his eyes kept wandering to Irene on the front pew near the piano. She had crept into his heart and his mind and lodged there.

At the close of the service, he got up and started down the aisle toward the door with his mother. Jolene Blake caught up to them and touched his arm. When he stopped and turned, she pressed a note into his hands. "Hope you can come," she whispered, and headed on across the room.

He looked down and read the note. It was an invitation. He smiled and looked over to see her hand a note to someone else. When she glanced back, he gave her a discreet nod.

Bright sunlight splashed through the drapes of Irene's bedroom, inviting her to wake and welcome the new day. She peeked through one eyelid, reluctant to abandon her pleasant dreams. Then she remembered the significance of the day. Not one person had mentioned her birthday all week.

Feeling neglected and perhaps a tad resentful, she forced herself out of bed. As soon as breakfast was over, she gathered the laundry and set to work. By midmorning she had the clothes on the line, the warm sun and a nice breeze drying them rapidly.

Her dad divided his time between tending the stock, fixing fences and tools, and working in the field. Today he plowed the garden spot. He came walking across the yard, his white hair gleaming. "Did Jolene say anything about supper tonight?"

Irene nodded. "I've been on the run all week and haven't seen her since Sunday at church. But she said back then that she expects us as usual."

"Then I just want a sandwich for lunch." He went to wash up to eat.

Irene brought the clothes in off the line after lunch and sprinkled the items that had to be ironed, thinking longingly of an electric washing machine and iron. As she finished, her afternoon piano students began to arrive.

"You ready to go?" Sam asked, pulling on his coat at about four o'clock.

"Soon as I put this away." She moved the basket of clothes to the back porch, out of the way. She had another late night of ironing by lamplight ahead of her. Before teaching school she had always washed on Monday and ironed on Tuesday, like most women she knew. But now she did it whenever she could.

Irene drove. When they got to the lane leading to Jolene and Riley's house, she looked up the low inclined hill and saw that the place was packed with cars, trucks and wagons. As she pulled closer, she recognized most of them. Gavin's truck was among them. Rayona's new car sat next to Juanita Tomlin's much older one. Now Irene knew what Jolene had done.

People spilled out of the house into the yard. As she and her dad got out of the car, they began to sing "Happy Birthday." She looked over at him. "You knew."

He shrugged. "I mighta."

She glanced down at her old navy-and-white-print dress with a white collar and wished she had worn a nicer one.

Jolene came marching toward them, Rayona behind her. "Happy twentieth, little sister." She gave Irene a big hug.

"You stinker, you." Irene accepted another hug from Rayona. "You wanted me to think you forgot."

Her sister grinned and took her hand. "Of course. Now come on in and have a good time."

Irene followed the group to the door but stopped to pat the head of Sandy, the light-colored dog that belonged to Riley. Inside the kitchen, Jolene had a huge layered birthday cake on the cabinet. A large wicker basket sat beside it. Jolene waved a hand at it. "Those are cards, notes and pictures for you to go through and enjoy later."

The table held food of all kinds, telling Irene that others had contributed.

"After we eat, the men will make ice cream to go with the cake."

Irene hardly knew what to do with so much attention focused on her. She faced her friends and neighbors. "Thank you all for coming. I hope you're all hungry."

Her eyes swept the group and found Gavin. Riley's aunt Lily, who lived in Springfield, was also there.

"There aren't enough chairs or space around the table," Jolene said to the group. "So let's have the blessing. Then you can fill your plates and eat wherever you can find a place. Our birthday girl will go first."

As soon as Riley blessed the food, Irene filled her plate, got a cup of coffee and started to the living room with it. As she did, she noticed that Juanita Tomlin had sidled up next to her dad in the line circling the table. The widow laughed up at him in a flirtatious way and placed a generous helping of stewed tomatoes on his plate, telling him that she had fixed it just the way she knew he liked it.

"I think she has her cap set for him."

The whisper near her ear made Irene whip her head back around. Gavin wore an impish grin.

Irene rolled her eyes. "I think you're right."

"Do you think it's mutual?"

She fought to restrain a snicker. "I know it's not. You better get a plate or you'll go hungry."

He chuckled and followed his family to the table. "No danger of that."

Irene found a seat at the end of the sofa and placed her coffee cup on the table next to her. A couple minutes later Aunt Lily sat beside her.

"You've grown into quite a young lady since I last saw you," the tall gray-haired widow said in her friendly way.

"The time has certainly flown."

"Jolene tells me you're filling in for her this year. What do you plan to do after school ends for the summer?" She sipped her coffee and eyed Irene over the brim of the cup.

"I'm hoping to find a job related to gospel music."

Aunt Lily put the cup down and pursed her lips in thought. "Hmm. Would you like for me to locate some addresses of music businesses in Springfield and send them to you?"

A smile burst from Irene. "That would be appreciated. Thank you."

Gavin's mother sat in the chair facing them. "The kids were upset when they first heard that your sister would not be their teacher this year, but they're real happy now. In fact, I think they hate for your year to end. They want both of you. Even Wesley, who never cared much for school, seems to like you."

That surprised Irene. "He's been better behaved lately. I'm proud of him."

"It's pretty outside, even if it is a bit nippy." The voice of one of the men drifted from the kitchen. "Why don't we go out on the back porch."

Minutes later the house held only women and small children. The atmosphere became something of a hen party, but Irene enjoyed the time with the women. Soon the men brought their plates to the kitchen and went back out to crank the ice-cream machines.

By the time everyone had had their fill of birthday cake and ice cream, the sky was beginning to turn dark. People began to repeat their birthday wishes and leave.

"Thanks for coming," Irene said to them all. To the children she added, "See you in the morning." Then she went to the kitchen to help with the cleanup.

"Oh, no, you don't." Jolene pushed her through the doorway. "You're the birthday girl. Go play."

Ordered away from the work, Irene got her coat from

the hallway closet and went outside. Only Riley, her dad
and Gavin remained in the yard. Gavin looked up from
dumping water out of a freezer and approached her as
she stepped off the porch.

"Hi, got a minute?"

She shrugged. "I'm not busy."

"Ordered off duty, huh?" His grin was boyish.

She returned it. "Afraid so."

He reached for her hand and drew her along with him
toward his truck. When they reached it, he released her
hand and opened the door. He reached behind the seat
and pulled out a sack. Then he turned back to face her.

"I...uh...I got you something for your birthday," he
blurted, as if nervous. "I hope you'll accept these." He
removed two packages from the sack and handed them
to her.

Unsure how to react, Irene stared at them. "What are
they?"

"Open them and see. That one first." He pointed at
the flat package.

She did and smiled at him. "Chocolate creams. How
did you know about my sweet tooth?"

"Doesn't everybody have one? Now open the other
one."

She tore off the paper and opened the box—and nearly
bounced with excitement when she found an electric iron.
"This makes it seem more real."

His smile widened. "That was the idea."

Irene stared at him, noting the small lines at the edges
of his eyes, the firm line of his mouth. Her voice caught
as she tried to speak. She tried again. "Thank you."

He opened his mouth but closed it. Then opened it
again. "The REA circus is going to be in the Springfield
area soon. Would you like to go?"

She tilted her head, unable to speak and hardly able to breathe. Her thoughts were so jumbled she wasn't sure she understood. "You...you want me to go with you?"

He nodded. "I'd like to take you."

"I'd love to go," she said honestly, and then hesitated. "But..."

"What?"

"Is it during the week?"

His smile dimmed. "Yes."

She bit her lip, thinking fast. This was such an opportunity. To see the co-op's farm show prior to getting electricity in their home would be wonderful. And to attend it with Gavin would be even more wonderful. "Maybe Jolene could fill in for me. How many days would it be?"

"It's usually two days."

"May I let you know after I talk to Jolene?"

His expression brightened. "Sure. Here comes your dad."

Irene watched him walk away, her heart fluttering out of control.

Chapter 10

"I am so jealous." Jolene pushed a rolling pin over the dough, shaping it to fit a pie pan. "I've been hearing about the REA Farm Equipment Tour ever since it started last year in Iowa. I sure would like to attend one of their stops."

Irene grinned and rocked baby Rolen in her arms. She had stopped by after school to ask Jolene about filling in for her at school so she could go. "It's become very popular. I understand that hundreds attend each day. I can't believe I get to go to one."

Jolene paused in crimping the crust around the edge of the pan. "I know you'll have a great time with Gavin. Although I think you would have a great time anywhere if you were with Gavin," she added with a meaningful lift of her brows.

Irene put the baby on her shoulder and patted his back. "Are you sure you don't mind filling in at school for me? This little guy will miss you."

Jolene waved a floury hand in dismissal. "I wouldn't have agreed to do it if I minded. Besides, I miss teaching, and the kids. It'll be fun to have some time with them. Riley's mom or Callie will be happy to babysit for me. They can get used to him before I have to let them take turns keeping him regularly this fall. I'm also sure that Aunt Lily would be happy for the two of you to stay overnight with her so you can attend both days of the show."

Irene hadn't thought of that, but the idea appealed to her. She looked around, wondering where the woman had gone.

"She went to town to meet her friend Josephine Molton for ice-cream sodas at the drugstore. She said she couldn't go home without seeing Josie. I'll talk to her about your trip when she gets home. Do you know the exact date?"

Irene shook her head. "Gavin just said next month."

"It's okay. Aunt Lily will welcome you anytime."

Irene read the certainty on her sister's face and decided to accept the plan if it suited Gavin. Telling Gavin that she had her absence covered gave her an excuse to see him, but she didn't have time today. She needed to get home and fix supper for her dad. "I read through my birthday cards and notes last night. They were touching. And the pictures the children drew were delightful. That basket was a wonderful gift. You have such good ideas."

"We have wonderful friends." Jolene placed the pies in the oven and rinsed her hands. "I didn't get around to telling you over the weekend, but Riley is doing some work for the contractor who is building the REA lines."

The baby burped, making Irene jump. "Doing what?"

"Digging post holes. He gets up extra early and milks the cows and then goes to town to meet the crew. He works ten hours and then comes home and does his work here. Things haven't been real busy at the mill, so this is a way to make some extra money. They pay thirty-five cents an hour, plus bonuses. But I'm afraid he'll work himself to death."

Irene frowned in question.

"If they dig more than ten holes a day, they earn a bonus for each extra hole in addition to their hourly wage."

Irene whistled. "That's powerful motivation. Knowing Riley, he's pushing for twenty."

"He just started the middle of last week. Friday he bragged that he had done fifteen and meant to do better today."

"Well, it's only until the lines are done," Irene pointed out. "He's strong. He'll be okay if it's only temporary."

She continued to pat the baby, who had gone to sleep. "Since you won't let me have this little fellow, I'll put him to bed. I'd better get home before Dad comes looking for me."

"Here, let me have him. You run along."

When she drove up to the house, Irene saw men in the field. Curious, she got out of the car and crossed the yard to stand by the fence. She could tell they were digging. Had Riley gone with another crew, or could he be working this close to home?

The sound of a motor drew her attention. She looked down the road and saw a truck coming on the far side of the field. As it rounded the corner toward the house, she recognized Gavin. She raised a hand in a signal for him to stop.

Gavin spotted Irene in her backyard. At a signal from her, he pulled to the side of the road, parked and got out of the truck.

"Jolene will teach for me, but she needs to know the exact date," she said as they met in the middle of the yard.

He couldn't keep from grinning. "Good. I checked the date today. Tell her Monday and Tuesday two weeks from now." He swept his eyes over her glowing face, glad that she had agreed to go with him and that she seemed excited about it. Of course, that excitement could be more about the show than him. But he didn't care.

"She said Riley's aunt Lily will let us spend the night at her house. She has plenty of extra room and loves to have company."

He had met the woman at Irene's birthday party, and Riley had talked about how he and Callie had each stayed with her when they needed to leave home to find work in the city. "That sounds good. I'll make arrangements at work." He glanced over at the field. "You keeping tabs on the workers?"

She grinned. "Jolene told me that Riley is digging holes. I was looking to see if he might be with this crew."

He moved toward where she had stood earlier, pleased when she accompanied him. "This is a fast-moving operation. The digging foreman loads up about eight men on a flatbed truck and hauls them to that day's work location. He drops one of them, along with his five-foot shovel and heavy-duty post-hole digger, at every sixth pole. When the worker has his five holes dug, he's moved to a new location on down the line."

She squinted across the field. "Not everyone out there is digging."

"Some of them are mechanics. Those stakes not only tell them where the holes should be, they tell the mechanics what hardware to attach to the poles."

When she went still and peered more intently, he followed her line of vision to where a man had raised his head and turned toward them. "Do you recognize someone?"

She craned her head forward, studying the man. "I think that's Zeke Lonigan," she said slowly, a note of something he couldn't quite identify entering her voice.

He looked closer. "I think you're right. I haven't seen the man in years, but he looks like what I remember. Didn't I hear that his boys got into some serious trouble?"

She nodded and faced him, her expression troubled. "They're in prison for stealing cars."

He remembered the general reputation of the family. "He's Zada's dad, right?"

"Yes. She said her dad has a new job, but she didn't say what. I hope it lasts…" Her words trailed to a halt.

"Longer than past ones?" he finished for her.

She inhaled a deep breath. "A lot of people think he was involved in the stealing with his boys, that he just didn't get caught, and they never told."

"Do you think he could be the petty thief who's been taking things from people's homes?"

The lines of her brow deepened.

"I wouldn't want to accuse him without proof," she said slowly. "But I think he bears watching."

"I agree. Good night, Irene," he sang in an off-key execution of a popular song while waving his hand and backing across the yard. Her trill of laughter reached deep inside him. He turned and sprinted for his truck and grinned like a cat all the way home. He couldn't remember when he had felt so good.

As he drove into the farmyard, he looked around for Wes—and spotted the boy shimmying up the trunk of the big oak tree at the side of the yard. No telling why.

Probably to see how fast he could do it, from the looks of him.

"Hey, Wes," he called as he got out of the truck. He reached into the back and got the extra tools he had borrowed from Dale. "If we hurry with chores and get back outside as soon as we eat, we might have enough daylight to get started on our doodlebug."

Wes slid down the tree and landed with a thump. He brushed his hands against his pants leg and came running. "Let's get going."

Gavin smiled inwardly at the improvement in the boy's attitude. No longer surly and argumentative, he seemed excited at their new project. Now to keep him too busy for pranks.

By the time they got the milking done and wood split and carried in for the night, Mom and the girls had supper ready. They ate quickly and went to the old car they had left down beside the barn.

"This is gonna be better than those poor old things Eddie Dawson and Gerald Foley ride all over the place," Wes bragged. "I can't wait to show 'em my backside."

Gavin grinned at the boy's excitement and competitive spirit. He hoped this new camaraderie that seemed to be developing between them lasted.

"I hope it can be used for more than just fun."

Wes nodded. "Eddie and Gerald say their dads use them for plowing, haying, hauling logs and pulling out stumps."

"We'll be sure to add a trailer hitch to the back of it."

He peered at the worn-out car that had once been the pride and joy of Mr. Harris and his wife, rubbing his chin. "I'm not sure where to start, so why don't we pick something easy to get us going."

Wes eyed it. "We're gonna take off as many metal parts as possible, ain't we?"

Gavin grinned. "Yep. I think I feel like tearing off a fender. You want the other one?"

A satisfying "Yes" came from Wes.

"Here, take this." He handed the boy a wrench.

They both went to work and soon had the fenders tossed aside. Gavin looked up at the darkening sky. "Let's see if we can get under it and take the muffler off before it gets too dark to see. I've got a flashlight in the seat of my truck, if you want to get it in case we need it to finish."

"Be right back." Wes spun and ran to get it.

Gavin crawled under the old car. He had to brush cobwebs from his face.

"Ugh, it's dirty under here," Wes snorted when he returned and crawled in beside him.

They worked together and got the job done. Gavin tossed the muffler on their junk pile and stood beside Wes to admire their project, both of them wearing happy grins. But then Wes faced Gavin, his expression turned serious. "Are you sorry you came back here to live?"

Gavin considered the question carefully. He wanted to be totally honest. "No, I'm not sorry. I missed Mom, and I'm getting to know you kids better."

"What about Mom wanting us to go to church so much? Don't you hate that?"

Again he wanted to be honest. He wiped his hands on a rag and gathered their tools. "At first I didn't want to go, but lately I've not minded so much. I've even been thinking I need to start reading the Bible."

Wes whipped his head around in surprise. "You have?"

Gavin nodded. "Yes, I have, and not just because it would please Mom. I think it would please God, and maybe help me become a better person. But my good intentions haven't gotten me anywhere yet. You interested in trying it?"

The boy's mouth twisted around a bit. "How about you try it and let me know if it helps you."

Now that aimed a direct challenge at him. He had to try, since he'd opened his mouth.

Aunt Lily's letter made Irene smile. Not only had the woman sent the promised list of addresses, but she had phrased her invitation for Irene and Gavin to stay with her during the farm show in decisive terms. She had everything planned.

As she read over the addresses again, Irene heard her dad come in the back door. He entered the living room a minute later, having shed his coat, and whacked his hat against his leg.

"It's starting to rain again, and that gang of men is out there with their pike poles and equipment to set the poles in place. They're making a mess of my fields, trying to drive that truck through the mud." His nostrils flared. "I've a mind to go out there and tell 'em to get out."

Irene listened as he aired his exasperation. The past two nights it had rained hard but had cleared up enough by morning for the men to work. She hated for anything to slow their progress.

"Maybe it'll stop raining and the ground will dry out over the weekend."

He snorted. "Maybe. Maybe not."

The sound of a vehicle pulling in outside interrupted them. He went to the window and peered out. "It's your friend Gavin Mathis. You better put on your pretty face."

Irene couldn't decide if he was teasing or being sarcastic because of Gavin's association with the electric company. She busied herself putting away Aunt Lily's letter in a table drawer while he went to the door.

"Hello, Mr. Delaney," Gavin greeted him. "I just stopped by to let you know that some of the residents are working on the lines with the crew. If you're interested in helping, you could make enough to get your house wired. I don't mean to meddle, sir. I just wanted to say something in case you're interested." His voice held a tinge of uncertainty.

Irene held her breath, wondering how Dad would respond. She also visualized Gavin's firm mouth and deep-set eyes.

"Thank you, Gavin," Dad said, as if he had not been spouting angry words minutes earlier. "I may stop in at the office and apply."

"Well, I need to go. I'm not done for the day, but I had to be in this area and thought I would stop. I plan to ask the foreman if he can figure out a way to get through those muddy fields without getting the pole truck stuck and tearing up the ground."

"I'd appreciate that," Sam said in a soft growl. "Thanks for stopping by."

Unable to stop herself, Irene went to the window and peeked through it. Just as she did, Gavin turned on the porch step and looked up, as if sensing her presence. Eyes locked on her, he executed a snappy wave—and winked. Then he turned and loped to his truck.

"Did you hear that?"

Irene whirled to face her dad, heat creeping up her neck at being caught at the window. "I heard. Are you interested?"

He nodded. "I think so. If I make enough money to pay for wiring the house, you could use what you have saved for some of the things you want."

Excitement washed through her. "A refrigerator?"

His mouth quirked. "A washing machine?"

She put down the spoon she held and wrapped her arms around him.

Gavin chuckled as he recalled the foreman's solution to the muddy field problem. The man had hitched a trailer to the truck and loaded a mule into it. Today when his crew got into a muddy location, he unloaded the mule, hitched it to a pole and let the big animal pull it into place for the pole setters.

After chores and supper that evening Gavin and Wes worked at stripping the body from the old car.

"Ouch!" Wes popped his thumb into his mouth.

Gavin looked up from working a door panel loose. "What did you do?"

Wes pulled the thumb out to speak. "Cut my thumb on a piece of metal."

"Let me help you." Gavin rounded the car and checked the thumb, thankful to see that it was just a small cut. "It'll smart awhile. You want to quit for the night?"

"No." Wes shook his head forcefully.

They worked until dark, then went inside and cleaned up. After the kids had gone to bed, Gavin joined his mother in the living room. As usual, she was reading her Bible.

"Is there another one of those around here?"

She looked up in surprise. "The kids each have one. I'll get Jennifer's for you." She went and got it and handed it to him. "You looking up something in particular?"

"No, I just thought, since you find it so interesting, I should read it, too." He wrinkled his nose at her.

She beamed.

He had no idea where to read, so he started at the beginning and read much later than he intended.

Over the next days he continued the pattern. He and Wes spent every minute he could squeeze from his schedule working on the doodlebug. Removing all the unnecessary parts and gadgets moved right along. But shortening the drive shaft to make a vehicle about the size of a small tractor proved more painstaking and time-consuming than they could do alone. Gavin enlisted the help of Riley Blake, whose experience doing handiwork around his dad's sawmill and farm and running the gas station in town had made him into a good mechanic.

Before going to bed each night, Gavin would begin his Bible reading where he had left off the night before. The stories of Adam and Eve, Cain and Abel, Noah, all held him in awe. The magnificence of God and all He had created filled him with emotion.

When they finished the doodlebug Saturday afternoon, they had nothing more than an engine and bench seat mounted on a short platform that rested on four wheels. Gavin handed Wes a key. "You ready for a driving lesson?"

The boy let out a whoop. "Sure am." He crawled up onto the seat of their odd-looking creation.

"Do you know how to drive?"

Wes peered down at the floorboard. "I think so."

Uh-oh. "How about we go over some things, just to be sure." He went over how to start it, stop it, and back up. Then he stood back to watch Wes press the starter button to the floor and release the hand brake.

With a loud roar Wes drove around the pasture behind the barn, laughing and yelling the whole time. Gavin had never seen the boy so happy. It warmed his heart.

When Wes finally stopped and got off, he wore a silly grin. "That was great. Now it's your turn."

Gavin enjoyed his turn almost as much as Wes had. When he parked and climbed off, the boy gave him a cocky grin. "You gonna take your girl for a ride in it?"

Without bothering to deny anything, Gavin reached out and gave the boy's head a knuckle rub. "I might."

Chapter 11

Irene's emotions swung from one extreme to the other. The sight of the truck, stringing conductors, linemen following to secure them and hang transformers raised her excitement to nearly unbearable heights. Her dad had been out there working all week, helping get the lines ready for service.

Yet her heart wrenched as she wrote letters to the companies on Aunt Lily's list. Leaving her home, especially now that there would be electricity to make life better, would be hard. But she had to go. She had a responsibility to use the talent God had given her for His ministry. Buried here in this small town, she had limited contacts and opportunities.

Uncertainties crept in. She had known since childhood that God had given her talent so she could serve Him. She had thought she would play for a singing group, but the only group she had was her uncle's little local group.

They sang at churches and community events, but they had homes and jobs here and would never travel and do evangelistic work.

What is Your plan for me, Lord?

Her future looked so blank. Why would God give her a talent and not give her a job that would utilize it? She couldn't just stay here and expect Dad to take care of her all her life.

Irene bent to her letter-writing task. The school year would be coming to an end. She had to explore every possibility.

Lord, if any of these places is where You would have me go, open the door. If not, show me what other direction I should look.

A knock sounded at the door as she put the letters in envelopes. She put them down and went to answer it.

Juanita Tomlin stood on the porch, her thick salt-and-pepper hair flying in the blustery March wind. In addition to her purse, she carried a notebook and pencil. Her eyes peered past Irene into the house. Irene managed to not snicker at the woman's obvious disappointment that Sam had not been the one to answer the door.

"Dad's not home from work yet. May I help you?"

Juanita stepped inside out of the wind. "Now that the electrical lines are getting close to time to be hooked up, we need to get our houses wired. A group wiring plan has been organized so we can do it cheaper. By joining together we can keep the cost to fifty-five dollars. Manufacturers are putting out lighting packages that contain nine fixtures for only about eighteen dollars. Would you like to join?"

Her voice had risen in pitch and gotten faster as she recited her little sales speech.

"It sounds good," Irene said. "But I'm not the one to do that. Dad is taking care of the wiring."

Juanita pursed her lips for a moment. "Tell Sam about the plan and that I'll be back later this evening so he can join the group."

Irene watched the woman return to her car and drive away. Juanita was a good woman, but not one she particularly relished having for a stepmother. But her dad would have to decide whether he wanted to remarry, and, if so, who it would be.

Unsettled at thinking about such possibilities, Irene went to the kitchen to start supper. She had it ready when Dad got home and persuaded him to eat before going to do chores. While they ate their simple meal of corn bread, ham, fried potatoes and apple butter, she told him about Juanita's visit.

He plunked his fork down on the table and ran a hand over his eyes. "I don't know what to do about that woman. She's always around, always meddling and always sneaking up on me."

"She's a hard worker and helps out with community projects," Irene pointed out.

He pushed his chair back. "I'm going to the barn. You can go ahead and sign us up. I'll be back after she's gone."

Irene restrained a laugh and began to clean up. As much as she hated explaining her dad's absence to Juanita, she delighted in signing the list for the wiring plan. It was really going to happen. They would have lights. Appliances. And more.

Gavin spent the week running all over the countryside, overseeing changes, checking safety procedures, resolving issues and then going back to the office to prepare his reports. By the time he got home late Friday he was so tired he didn't see how he could manage one more chore. But he still had to see that the cow was milked and wood split and carried in for the night. He longed for the day when his family would have power to make some of their work easier.

Mom met him at the door. "Wes already milked. He's splittin' wood now."

He tried not to show his relief. "I'll go help him."

"He can do it. You're beat."

Gavin shook his head. "It's already dark. He needs to get done." He headed out the back door.

"I got enough cut for the front room. Just need kitchen wood now," Wes said as Gavin joined him at the wood-pile.

"Why don't you carry that in and give me the ax."

Wes handed it over and gathered an armload of wood. His lack of complaint and his willingness to go ahead with chores alone amazed Gavin. *Thank you, God.*

When they gathered the last of the wood to take it inside, Wes scooped some items off a big chunk of wood and placed them atop his load.

"Whatcha got there?"

"Just some old wire I found when I was out walkin' in the fields."

"You mean where the electrical crews have been working?"

The boy gave him a wide-eyed look. "Yeah. I found pieces of little colored wires on the ground and wrapped 'em around these sticks. Weren't nothin' wrong with pickin' 'em up, was there?"

Gavin shrugged. "I guess not, so long as it's at places where they're done working."

"I'm not the only one does it."

"What do you mean?" Gavin opened the door and held it for Wes to go in ahead of him.

"I saw Zeke Lonigan out behind the Dixons' house yesterday when I was walkin' home from school. He had a wad of it in his hands."

They dumped their loads in the wood box. Gavin sniffed the air. "Something smells good."

"We're having chicken and dumplings, green beans and stewed tomatoes," his mother informed them from the stove.

Gavin closed his eyes and inhaled deeply. "And pie?"

She grinned. "There's a blackberry cobbler in the oven. Get washed up and we'll eat." She pointed at the red iron pump at the long, shallow sink.

They didn't have to be told twice.

Gavin stopped at the church door after service to wait for Irene to emerge. His mother gave him a knowing look, smiled and ushered the kids on to the truck. "I'll be there in a couple of minutes," he said after her.

When Irene and her sister appeared, Jolene also smiled, said goodbye and kept going.

"Hi," he said quietly, suddenly tongue-tied. He didn't understand the effect Irene had on him. "Can you be ready to leave by seven in the morning?"

Their eyes held for a timeless moment. Then she smiled. "I'll have my bag packed. I told Aunt Lily not to expect us until sometime in the evening."

He watched her walk to her car. Getting the next two days off had required some tough negotiations and labor. He had worked extra hours to get some jobs finished that his boss insisted could not be delayed and had committed to more extra hours after he got back. He also had agreed to pick up a box of chocolates for the boss's wife. But these two days with Irene would be worth it—and more.

The afternoon passed quickly. After dinner he went out to split some extra wood to give Wes a head start on the needs for the next couple of days. He was just finishing when a car pulled into the lane beside the yard. Leon Gentry got out and started to the porch. When he glanced over and spied Gavin, he veered toward the woodpile.

"Howdy, Gavin." He extended a palm for a firm handshake as they met halfway.

"Hello, Leon. You out for a friendly Sunday-afternoon visit?"

The marshal's eyes crinkled at the corners. "I'm afraid not. I stopped by to ask if you've seen anything that might help me catch our petty thief."

"More reports?"

He nodded. "The Dixons talked to me a while ago. Said they got some canned stuff and a side of pork missing."

Gavin's eyes narrowed as his gut tightened. "When?"

Leon eyed him sharply. "Sometime yesterday afternoon or last night. What is it?"

Gavin drew a deep breath and raked a hand over the back of his neck. "Wes mentioned seeing…"

"Spit it out, man. You're not accusing anyone."

He swallowed the obstruction in his throat. "Wes said he was exploring in the fields and collecting scraps of wire left behind by the line crews when he saw Zeke Lonigan behind the Dixon place."

Leon shook his head. "I can't say I'm surprised. Is Wes here?"

"He rode the doodlebug over to the Lonigan place to see Zada."

"I see. Okay, I'll take your word that he saw Zeke. That

way, if I have to arrest the man, Wes won't have told me anything. And this conversation will stay private if I can find a way to confirm the identity of our thief without involving Wes."

"Thanks."

Irene packed an overnight bag with a change of clothes and a nightgown. Then she added her tube of Ipana toothpaste and a personal bar of Lifebuoy soap. As she worked, she decided to act on something that had been floating around in her mind all week.

She got out her writing supplies and sat down at the kitchen table. It was a lofty idea to think that the Hartford Music Institute would consider her for their faculty. But what did she have to lose beyond the expense of a letter? When she finished writing it, she put it in her purse.

That evening before bedtime she heated water and took another tub bath in the kitchen. Then she rewashed her hair, even though it was still clean from the previous night's cleaning.

It still amazed her that she was preparing to go on a trip that was a date with a man. She had gone on a few dates, but none of them had ever made a lasting impression on her. This time her heart and mind were deeply affected.

She woke early the next morning, too excited to sleep any later. She had breakfast ready when her dad entered the kitchen. He had not objected when she asked him to eat before going to do chores just this once so she could feed him before leaving.

As soon as they finished eating, Sam got up. With a little grin tugging at his mouth, he said, "Have fun," and left the house.

Irene cleaned the kitchen and dashed to her room to

get dressed. She put on a simple white blouse, a navy skirt and a light blue cardigan. Then she brushed her hair and pulled it back from her face with the ends turned under.

After dabbing a little toilet water on her neck, she placed the bottle in the bag with her other things. Then she gathered her coat, purse and the bag and went to the porch swing to wait for Gavin. Within minutes his truck came up the road and pulled in at the house.

Her heart rate quickened as she got up and met him at the porch steps. He looked comfortable, and way too handsome, in a white shirt, denim pants and a denim jacket.

"Let me take that." He reached for her bag.

She passed it to him and didn't resist when he placed her hand on his arm to escort her to the truck. He assisted her up into it. She brushed her skirt into place and tucked her purse below her feet while he closed the door and went around the truck and got behind the wheel.

He looked across the seat, his eyes sweeping over her in detail. "You look...*very* nice."

"Thank you." This felt so good, too good. She shouldn't like Gavin so much. She needed to keep her focus, find out how to honor God with the talent He had given her.

Irene sat stiffly as Gavin backed the truck out and headed toward town, not sure how to act now that she was alone with him. She took a deep breath as they passed the Miller place. "Did you know that Bob lost his farm while you were living away from here?"

He glanced over at her. "But he lives there now, doesn't he?"

She nodded. "You know about the penny auctions?"

His mouth dimpled at the corners. "You mean when farmers used threats and violence to convince buyers not to bid more than a few cents on foreclosed farms?"

She nodded. "Yes. That way the original owner could buy back his farm and equipment for almost nothing, saving his land."

"Bob did that, huh?"

"He sure did."

"That's hard to visualize. I remember Bob as a mild-mannered man."

"He is, but desperation makes a man do desperate things." As she talked, Irene began to relax and enjoy chatting with him. Talk of school, their families, community news and other inconsequential matters made the time fly.

When they arrived at a large field where two huge tents stood, Gavin turned into the lane leading to an adjoining huge field where cars were parked.

Irene leaned forward to take in the sight. "It really does look like how I imagined a circus would look."

She had heard about how the REA hauled their demonstration equipment across the country in a caravan of trucks and set up their big tents, leading people to start calling the show the REA circus.

Gavin found a spot to park and turned off the truck motor. He turned to face her, wearing a wide grin. "The long narrow tent will be the appliance tent, the square-shaped one the auditorium tent. It looks like they're barely set up and already drawing a big crowd."

"Good. We'll have plenty of time to explore."

He opened his door and rounded the truck by the time she got hers open. As he helped her down, he wove his fingers through hers and led her across the field amid a flock of people.

Irene gazed around, trying to absorb it all. "I can see why you like working for this company. Do you plan to move back to the city when your mother doesn't need you so much?"

"I don't think so. At least not so long as my job is okay."

They spent what remained of the morning strolling about the grounds. Then they stopped and ate lunch at one of the cook tents run by women's groups using the latest electric appliances brought to the show by the REA home economists. As they finished eating, music could be heard coming from beyond the cook tent.

Gavin nodded toward the auditorium tent. "Sometimes country musicians play free shows before the demonstrations. Want to go in there?"

"Of course. I want to see and do everything."

They made their way to the "big top" and found a place to sit on one of the hard benches that were already nearly full of happy spectators. A young singer occupied the stage, strumming a guitar and belting out a song.

Following his performance came lectures and demonstrations on lighting and wiring. When it ended, they both stood.

"My whole body is stiff," Irene said, but her smile belied any complaint.

"Mine, too." Gavin's eyes met hers. "I assume you want to get some of the printed materials from the information booth."

"Of course." Her response bubbled with excitement.

After collecting copies of everything available, they browsed through the appliance tent and ate again before returning to the auditorium tent.

The evening show featured a home electrification specialist who demonstrated how to put together electric light fixtures with pull chains or wall switches.

"This has been great, and tomorrow sounds every bit

as good," Irene said with enthusiasm as they drove to Aunt Lily's after the show. "Thank you for bringing me."

He smiled over at her. "Thank you for coming."

Aunt Lily met them at the door. "There's food in the warmer if you're hungry."

Irene shook her head. "Even if I were, I'm too tired to eat."

"Same here. Thank you for having us, Mrs. Adams."

A thin woman, Aunt Lily radiated a calm and confident demeanor. She had married young and lost her husband to influenza months later. Then she had lost the baby she was carrying. She had never remarried and had become a bank teller. She still worked and claimed she would continue to do so until forced to quit.

"I've made a small bedroom of my screened back porch. You may sleep there, Gavin. Irene will have the spare bedroom upstairs."

Within minutes the house had grown silent.

The next morning Irene put on the dress she had brought. It had an A-line shape, with small red anchors patterned on a gray background, with matching red trim on the bolero.

Over breakfast Aunt Lily asked all kinds of questions, and they told her all about their day.

"I'm glad you came by, even if it was a short visit," she said as they parted ways at the porch, Aunt Lily to work and the two of them back to the show.

Midmorning they watched demonstrations of how electric washers, dryers and stoves worked. In the afternoon they were shown small appliances, refrigerators, freezers and what could be done with automatic water pumps that made indoor plumbing possible. They also saw electric brooders for chickens, poultry-house lighting and dairy-farm equipment. The evening cooking show seemed to be the most popular event of the entire show.

"This has made me greedy," Irene said as they headed back to the truck to start home. "I want everything."

Gavin reached over and clasped her hand in his. "You look happy."

She nodded and aimed a wistful glance back over her shoulder. "I am. My mind can't grasp all the possibilities."

As they walked away from the lights, the world seemed to grow smaller. Her hand in Gavin's made Irene's heart hammer like some of the machines she had seen. She missed it when he released her once she was in the truck seat. She sat in silence while he went around and got in beside her.

The wonders of the past two days filled her mind as the miles melted away. But the wonder of all the powers she had seen were nothing compared to the power that held her in its grip.

She loved Gavin.

Chapter 12

As the miles rolled away, Irene's eyes began to droop. She was not used to this wild nightlife, and she had to get up early in the morning to go to school. Losing the fight to stay alert, she sagged back in the seat, and the world went quiet.

She woke with a start when the truck stopped. And was further startled when she realized that her head lay against Gavin's shoulder. Awake now, she pushed her hair back over her ears and sat bolt upright. "Sorry I went out on you like that."

"Don't be sorry. You were tired and needed the rest." His voice was soft in the near-total darkness.

She reached for the door handle. "I had a wonderful time."

"So did I. I'd like to spend more time with you like that." His arm slid across the back of the seat and touched her shoulders. "Could I take you for a ride sometime this coming weekend?"

Her hand slipped from the door handle. She turned and found his face closer than she expected. For a moment she couldn't breathe. His breath blew softly across her temple. "That sounds like fun," she said in a shallow voice, even as her brain warned against it. *I'm leaving.*

Irene blinked and sat motionless as his arm drew her to him. Then he leaned forward, and his lips brushed over hers in a gentle, searching kiss. Paralysis gripped her.

I'm leaving, her brain repeated.

But right now I want this.

As his mouth bestowed the most tender kiss imaginable, her arms crept up around his neck. When it ended, she forced herself to move away from him.

"I don't really want to leave," he said in a low whisper. "But I know you have to get some rest so you won't fall asleep at school tomorrow."

His voice in the dark night, the caress of his warm breath on her cheek, made it next to impossible to leave him. But with her mind clearing a bit, she edged toward the door.

He got out of the truck and came around to open it for her. He helped her out, took her bag and walked with her to the house.

She turned to face him. "Thank you for everything. You could not have chosen an outing that I would have enjoyed more."

"I'd like to kiss you again," he said quietly. "But I'm afraid to press my luck. But be warned that I probably won't be able to exercise such restraint this weekend."

She grinned at the mock severity in his voice and did her best to ignore the inner trembling caused by his threat. "I'll practice my survival skills until then."

"Have a good week, Irene."

"Good night, Gavin." She took her bag from him, went inside the house and peeked behind the curtains to watch him go back to his truck and drive away. Gavin was a threat to her peace of mind. Thoughts of him kept her awake at night.

He had a quality of sincerity, the way he had come home to look after his family, the commitment to doing his job well, that touched deep inside her. She knew he had become disillusioned as a teenager and drifted away from his Christian life. But he seemed to be resolving his issues with God and reaching out to others. How could she resist him?

How can I leave him?

In bed a few minutes later she remembered that she had not mailed her letter to the music institute. She would put it in the mailbox on her way to school in the morning.

Thursday morning Irene's heart sank as she took roll and noted that while one of the Holman girls had been present yesterday, all three were absent today. What could be wrong? The girls seemed fine when they were here. The ones present never said that whoever was absent was sick. They just said Mom needed help or made some other vague excuse. Irene had offered to go talk to their mother, but they insisted that was not necessary. What more could she do?

Irene forced worries about the girls—and memories of last night's kiss—to the back of her mind and proceeded with classes.

During recess she stood in front of the school and watched the younger children play games alongside the building. The older ones had a baseball game going in the huge yard behind the school. Suddenly loud laughter and yelling came from back there. Irene hurried around the building to see what had happened.

The students stood in a semicircle, watching something between the two big walnut trees several feet from the fence line. As she got near, Irene saw Wesley sprawled on the ground.

"What's going on?" she asked, practically yelling to be heard over their laughter and chatter.

"He got a dose of his own medicine," someone said with a howl.

Irene dropped to her knees beside Wesley. "Are you hurt?"

He stared up at her, his face flushed. "I tripped."

"On the trip wire he rigged between the trees to see one of us take a tumble." Henry Warren, a sixth grader, pointed at the broken wire lying nearby. "He was chasing a fly ball and forgot he put it there."

More laughter erupted.

Wesley rolled over and got to his feet, hobbling on one foot. His mouth worked around in a little dance of embarrassment. "I guess it wasn't very funny," he muttered.

Irene folded her arms and gave him a stern look. "Do you understand now that your pranks can be dangerous as well as not funny to the victims?"

His chin dropped nearly to his chest. "Yeah."

She debated whether further punishment was warranted but decided against it. He seemed genuinely chastened. "I hope there won't be any more pranks, then. You're too old to risk injuring your friends."

"Yes, ma'am."

She sighed. *Thank you, Lord, for getting us through another lesson.*

"Recess is over. Go inside and get out your history books."

* * *

Thursday evening Gavin had just arrived home from work and was getting out of the truck when the marshal's car pulled in behind him. Leon Gentry got out and came to meet him.

"Have you seen Zeke Lonigan hanging around?" he asked without preliminaries.

"No. What's up?"

Leon shook his head in resignation. "A couple of people recognized him leaving their places and found things missing. I'm looking for him to arrest him. He's not at home, and his wife claims to have no idea where he is. She did admit that he lost his job last week."

"I haven't seen him, and Wes hasn't mentioned him again."

Leon touched the brim of his hat. "Well, if you do, will you let me know?"

"Sure will."

Gavin hated what the man's arrest would mean to his wife and daughters, who still lived at home, but he couldn't be allowed to steal from his neighbors, even if it was to feed his family. And he knew in his heart that the daughters did not want to live that way.

Friday morning Wesley entered the school and took his seat in subdued silence. Had yesterday's incident upset him that much?

Irene watched the boy all morning. Instead of brightening, he seemed to become more depressed. During lunch in the schoolyard he nibbled at his sandwich and put half of it back in his lunch pail. Then he stood from the step where he had been sitting and headed around the school building toward the outhouse.

Minutes later when she rang the bell to signal the end

of lunchtime, a twinge of worry struck Irene that Wesley had still not returned. She decided to check on him. "Go ahead and get ready for arithmetic," she called to the students filing past her. "I'll be there in a minute."

She hurried around the side of the building, looking for the boy. Seeing no sign of him, she continued on toward the outhouse, wondering what to do. But she drew up short at the sight of Wesley sitting on the ground, slumped against the back of the building. If she was not mistaken, he had been crying.

She rushed over and knelt beside him. "What's wrong, Wesley? Is there anything I can do to help?"

He slowly lifted his face, his eyes shiny. His mouth trembled.

Irene took his hand in hers. "Did being made fun of yesterday hurt your feelings so much?"

He shook his head slowly back and forth.

"Then tell me what's wrong. I can't help if I don't know what's bothering you."

He opened his mouth but closed it. Then he swallowed and sat upright. "Zada says she's not coming back to school."

"What? Why?"

He drew a shuddering breath and glanced upward. "Her dad was arrested last night for stealing from the neighbors. Her brothers are already in prison. She says she can't face her friends anymore. She's afraid everyone will make fun of her and be mean to her. But she's a good girl, Miss Delaney. She works hard and studies hard."

"I know she does, Wesley." She thought a moment. "Will you go with me to see her after school?"

He lowered his gaze to meet Irene's. "You'll talk to her, get her to come back to school?"

"I'll try. But right now we need to get inside and start class. Okay?"

He gave her a hopeful smile, blinked and got to his feet.

That afternoon the boy remained subdued, but he paid attention and participated in class. As soon as Irene dismissed the students to go home, he told his siblings to go on without him and tell their mom why he would be late. Then he tackled Zada's janitorial duties. By the time Irene was ready to leave, he had the room clean and neat, everything ready for class Monday morning.

When she drove up to the Lonigan house, Irene had to swallow a lump of aversion at the sight of the junk-cluttered yard and porch, cracked windows and tattered screens. Zada always kept herself neat and clean in spite of the lack of encouragement at home. The girl had so much promise. She simply had to stay in school.

Irene prayed as she knocked on the door. *Lord, please give me the right words to say.*

Zada opened the door and stared out at Irene. Then her face took on a white pallor when she spotted Wesley behind her.

"May we talk to you?" Irene asked, wishing she could take the girl in her arms and make everything right for her.

Zada glanced behind her, and then stepped out onto the little square porch, probably not wanting her teacher to see more clutter, or her mother to hear their conversation.

"Do you mind sitting here on the porch?" she asked quietly.

"This will be fine." Irene sat on the edge of the wooden planks and secured her skirt around her legs, hoping to make Zada comfortable enough to listen to reason.

Zada sat beside her, hands folded in her lap. "I guess you want to talk about me quitting school."

"That's right. You need to finish the year and go on to high school. You're an excellent student with a bright future ahead of you. The other students and I miss you and want you there."

"But they'll…" She paused and bit her lip.

"No one will make fun of you or be mean to you," Wes spoke up fiercely. "Everybody knows what kind of person you are."

"He's right," Irene added. "We're sorry about your dad, but no one blames you for anything or thinks any less of you."

A tear trickled down the girl's cheek. Then she threw herself into Irene's arms. "Are you sure, Miss Delaney?"

Irene squeezed Zada to her, unable to speak past the lump in her throat. "I'm sure."

"We're sure," Wesley added, his fists clenched on his knees.

Zada lifted her face, her eyes shining with unshed tears. "Thank you both for coming. I don't really want to quit, but I was embarrassed and afraid."

"Well, don't be." Irene placed a thumb against the girl's cheek and wiped at the wet trail. "We need you. We depend on you."

Ever so slowly a smile came to Zada's face. "I wish I could do something for you."

Irene grinned. "As a matter of fact, you can. I'm concerned about Thelma, Velma and Selma Holman. They've been missing more and more school. Today they were all absent. Can you tell me what the problem is?"

A furrow creased Zada's brow. "I don't know, but I'll go see them tomorrow and try to find out, if that's what you want me to do."

"I'd appreciate it." Irene gave the girl another hug and got to her feet. "See you Monday?"

Zada nodded. "Bye, Miss Delaney. Bye, Wes." The last was said in a shy, soft tone.

After chores Saturday morning, Gavin went to the barn and started the doodlebug.

"Hey, you taking my buggy?" Wes peeked around the doorway of the stall where they stored the machine. His smile belied the scolding words.

So much for sneaking away.

"Thought I'd take a ride, check it out."

The boy smirked. "It's a real smart buggy. If you drive up to the road, it'll go right to Miss Delaney's house on its own."

"Go find something to do and mind your own business." Gavin backed through the barn doorway and drove out of the lot.

"Don't get lost," Wes called after him.

The teasing might have rankled a bit, but Gavin was glad to see Wes's spirits improved. Their talk last night had been encouraging. The kid was growing up.

When he pulled in at the Delaney house, Irene came around the side of the yard, drawn by the loud roar of the doodlebug. She wore a black-and-white-print dress and a huge smile that matched the sunny day. But she always looked good to him, no matter what she wore or in what kind of weather. He turned off the motor.

"Are you trying to scare away all the animals?" she accused, eyeing the machine in amusement.

He got off and walked to where she stood. "Yep. What are you doing?"

"Hanging up wet clothes."

"If I help you get it done, would you have time to take my chariot for a little drive?"

She examined it in speculation. "You trust me to drive your precious chariot?"

"I'm confident you can handle it." He loved being able to put that sparkle in her eyes.

"Then let's get busy." She whirled and headed back to the clothesline. He followed.

"I want to thank you for the way you handled Wes and Zada yesterday," he said as she took a dress from the basket of wet clothing on the ground and gave it a snap.

"I find Wes's concern for Zada touching. I hope she returns to school Monday as promised."

He took the dress from her and two pins from the bag dangling from the line and attached the dress to the line. "She will, but only because you went to see her. I think Wes is maturing and has developed his first affair of the heart. It will be interesting to see how long it lasts. I appreciate your patience with him."

She turned away from him and hung up a wet shirt, obviously flustered at his compliment. Which further endeared her to him. As she pinned another of her dad's shirts on the line, he reached for another item from the basket.

She spun around and pushed his hand aside. "I think I should do this myself. There might be some…uh…personal items in there." A twinkle appeared in her dark eyes.

Now it was his turn to be flustered. "Oh, okay." He backed away, a palm raised. "Sorry. I only meant to help."

Her laughter sounded musical to his ears. He crossed his arms and grinned at her. "Do I have to turn my back?"

"You have to go back to your chariot." She put a teasing emphasis on the last word.

He did as ordered and perched on the seat. Minutes later Irene came around the side of the house. When she saw him, she began to sing "Swing Low, Sweet Chariot" in her rich contralto voice.

He hopped to the ground and held out a hand. "My chariot awaits you, madam."

She stopped singing and gave it another visual appraisal. "Are these things as handy as people claim?"

"Young people love to run all over the neighborhood with them, but older folks don't like the racket they make. Wes and I have pulled out a couple of stumps with this one, and he likes to pull things around with it. But I guess the truth is we like to ride around in it for fun."

"Then I guess I should find out how much fun it is." She raised a foot to mount it.

Gavin clasped her arm and assisted her into the seat. Then he gave her some brief instructions. When the engine started with its usual roar, she clapped her hands over her ears.

"There's no muffler," he explained with a shout. "I'll ride back here." He stepped up onto the framework and gripped the back of the seat.

She took off with a lurch and drove in a circle around the huge front yard. "It *is* fun," she yelled over her shoulder, laughing.

"Told you," he yelled back, leaning forward so his face came near her ear. He wished he had the nerve to kiss her.

Ker-thump.

The bug hit something and bucked sharply. Distracted, he lost his footing and tumbled backward. He lay on the ground, winded.

The motor stopped. Seconds later Irene was at his side. She placed her hands on each side of his face. "Gavin, are you hurt?"

Not wanting her to remove her hands, he lay still.

"Gavin, speak to me. Tell me you're all right."

His chest tightened sharply as he inhaled her pleasant, soapy scent. Carefully he eased one eye open just enough to peer up at her.

She jumped to her feet. "Gavin Mathis, you are a phony. Get up from there right now."

Uh-oh. Caught. He sat up and held out a hand. "Help me up? Please?"

She rolled her eyes and shook her head. Then she grabbed his hand and gave him a sharp boost to his feet. "I think we've had enough fun now. I've got more clothes to wash."

Chapter 13

As she took her place at the piano Sunday morning, Irene reflected, or continued to reflect, about Gavin's trip to the house yesterday. He had seemed genuinely sincere in his approval of the way she had dealt with his little brother and the Lonigan girl. But it hadn't been necessary to make a special trip to see her and tell her.

Why did he fascinate her so? His tall handsomeness and friendly ways were certainly admirable. And he had demonstrated patience and caring toward his family and people of the area that he came into contact with in the course of his work. The kiss they had shared after their trip to Springfield had addled her brain. She had prayed about it and asked God to help her keep focused on her work rather than daydreaming, but her mind still wandered.

She propped a hymnbook on the piano and sat on the stool. *I'm trying to trust You, Lord, but I don't under-*

*stand all these new emotions pulling at me. Please di-
rect my path.*

As she finished the prayer, choir members began to fill
the pews behind the pulpit. She flipped the hymnal open
to the page that was to be their opening song—and nearly
fell off the stool when she saw Gavin enter the church
and make his way up the aisle to the pew near the front
where she always sat when the song service had ended.

Why was he seeking her out, spending so much time
with her? Could he be as helplessly drawn to her as she
was to him? He couldn't be. That was impossible.

Automatically she began to play a prelude, her fingers
skimming over the keys without conscious thought. She
missed a note at the sight of Juanita Tomlin marching up
the aisle and slipping into the pew that Sam usually occupied during services. Why did people tend to be such
creatures of habit that others could predict their behavior
and do this kind of thing?

Irene tried to concentrate on her playing, but she
missed another note as she watched the little drama being
played out before her, so subtly that no one else in the
auditorium paid any attention to it.

Her dad entered through the side door, still convers-
ing with one of the men from the Sunday school class he
taught. Irene could tell by his ever so slight pause exactly
when he spotted Juanita. Still listening to whatever Mr.
Brown was saying to him, he responded briefly to the
man before they parted. Then, without looking toward
"his" pew or indicating in any way that he had noticed
Juanita, he stopped at a pew across the aisle and sat beside Gavin's mother.

As Irene missed yet another note, her gaze darted to
Gavin. Had he noticed? Without smiling or moving his

head, he communicated with the slightest wink that
he had.

Irene forced her attention back to her music and finished the piece just as the song leader stepped to the
pulpit and asked the congregation to turn to page twenty-
five.

When the song service ended, she slid off the stool
and went to sit in the pew beside Gavin, leaving a careful
distance between them. The corners of his mouth twitching, he reached into the pocket of his white shirt and ex-
tracted a small notebook and pencil. Then he flipped to
the back page of it and began to write. He placed the note
on the pew and pushed it toward her.

Without picking it up, Irene read what it said: "My
mom and your dad?"

Irene gave a light shrug and looked up at the ceiling.
But then her sense of humor surfaced. To keep from be-
traying herself, she placed a hand over her mouth.

Gavin picked up the notepad and wrote again.

This time she read quickly. "Mom will protect him."

What else would Nell do? Was it possible that her dad
and Gavin's mom could become more than friends? The
very idea seemed odd. Crazy.

He wrote again. "Will you and Sam come to dinner
with us?"

She wrote back. "Jolene's expecting us. Pay attention."

Mouth twitching, he focused on the preacher.

Monday morning Irene stifled a giggle as she emptied the contents of her book satchel onto the desk and
recalled the good-natured teasing her dad had endured
yesterday afternoon at Jolene's house. He hadn't even
bothered to deny that he liked Mrs. Bozeman.

"She's a good woman who minds her own business,"

had been his response when Riley asked what Sam thought about her.

Irene hadn't fared so well when asked about Gavin. She had admitted to liking him but tried to make light of it. She and Dad had finally teamed up and told Jolene and Riley that they would be informed in good time if anything serious should develop in either relationship.

Her thoughts returned to the present when she looked at the clock and saw that Zada should have arrived ten minutes ago. Had the girl changed her mind about returning to school?

Irene went outside and stood on the top step in front of the door to watch for the girl. Soon students began to arrive. She mentally clicked off the roll as they went inside to deposit their lunch pails and came back out to play in the schoolyard before classes.

It was almost time to ring the bell when she spotted four figures coming up the road, one taller and the other three shorter. The smaller ones had to be the Holman girls. As they got nearer, she breathed a sigh of relief. It was them, all three of them. And the taller one was Zada.

Thank you, Lord.

Only when they got to the schoolyard did she notice that they were barefoot, all four of them.

In a sudden burst of insight she understood.

"You're just in time," she greeted them. "Put your lunch pails away and go ahead and take your seats."

Zada paused next to Irene as the three small girls went inside. She spoke softly. "Their shoes wore out. They were taking turns wearing the ones they had left. When the last pair wore out, they all stopped coming. They were too proud to explain, and their mother didn't want other kids to make fun of them."

Irene looked down at Zada's bare feet. "You found a

way to handle it. I'm so proud of you." She gave the girl a quick hug.

As Zada went on inside, Irene rang the bell. Students charged past her into the building, their voices cheerful and loud. When they took their seats, the room became silent.

Irene went to the front of the room and checked her roll sheet. Then she stepped aside while Zada led the students in the Pledge of Allegiance. When they settled back into their seats and began their reading lesson, she took her own seat. But soon she became aware of furtive movements about the room. On closer inspection she realized what was happening. Students were quietly and unobtrusively removing their shoes. When Wesley looked around and saw what was happening, he didn't move for several moments. Then he quietly followed suit and removed his shoes.

Irene now had a roomful of barefoot students. The sight brought tears to her eyes. She was tempted to take off her own but decided the teacher should probably not do that. But it didn't matter. What the students had done on their own had taught a far deeper lesson than anything she could teach them.

As April turned to May, Irene's excitement grew along with the children's. School would end soon, and they would be free for the summer. Some would work in the fields as hard as any hired hands, while others would have the freedom to roam and hang out with their friends.

Poles dotted the landscape all across the countryside, with the wires strung between them providing a new roosting place for a host of birds. Houses had been completely wired for weeks, as had the school and church. Fixtures were hung and bulbs in place, ready for the hour when the line would be energized. Many people had electric appliances already installed and ready for operation.

Irene had concentrated on a refrigerator, since they could afford but one appliance at a time. She knew how badly her dad wanted an electric radio, but he insisted that paying for the wiring was all they could do now. He would get along with his battery-operated one a little longer.

Irene was torn. These wonderful changes were exciting, but knowing she would have to leave them behind saddened her. She had begun to get polite letters from the companies she had written to about a job, each indicating they had nothing to offer her. But she knew there had to be something out there for her.

She wanted to serve God. See people come to know Him. Be part of a wonderful ministry. She had to move on when the time came.

Irene rushed straight home from school the day the electric company had said they would finally have electrical power.

"You've turned every switch on and off a dozen times." Dad's mouth quivered at the mock admonishment.

Irene stopped in the act of reaching for the bare bulb at the end of the wire hanging from the kitchen ceiling. She released the pull chain and glared at him. "So have you."

He shrugged and grinned. "But not the refrigerator."

A spontaneous laugh burst from her. And as she laughed, the bulb took on a dim glow. She held her breath and stared, mesmerized.

"Here it comes."

The excitement in her dad's voice made Irene dance up and down in the middle of the floor, her fists clenched in the air. She continued to stare as the dim glow gradually grew brighter, and then the room was bathed in light. Her heart squeezed with emotion, and she swiped a hand across her eyes. Then she spun around, her body quivering with excitement, and wrapped her arms around her dad. She pulled him in a whirl around the room.

"We have lights. We have power," she chanted over and over.

Suddenly she stopped. They grinned at one another and then raced in opposite directions. While Sam went to the living room and turned on the light, Irene ran to the refrigerator and pulled the door open. The sight of the little light glowing inside made it impossible to repress her tears any longer.

Her dad returned to the room. "It's good to hear you laugh." He opened his arms.

She ran into them. "I'm so happy, Dad. This will make our lives better, easier."

He gazed down into her eyes, his expression serious. "Does that mean you plan to stay here and enjoy the changes?"

She frowned, troubled at the conflicting uncertainties rushing through her. "I don't know what's ahead for me, Daddy. If I don't find a job, you may be stuck with me. I've told God I'm willing to do whatever He wills, but I don't know yet what He has planned for me."

Dad nodded, taking a few moments to speak. "I wish I could keep you with me always, but you're grown up now and have to follow your heart and God's calling. I understand, though. Remember the promise in Psalm 32:8. God says He will instruct and guide you in the way you should go." He gave her another squeeze and released her.

The next morning Irene was surprised to see Gavin's truck parked in front of the school when she arrived. As he got out of it, all she could think about was the kiss they had shared. It shouldn't have been such a big deal, but it was.

She pushed a stray lock of hair back from her face and got out of the car.

"I wanted to see your face this morning when you turn on the light here at school," he said when they met.

She pretended nothing had changed, that her stomach felt steady rather than like a tumbling pile of leaves caught in a whirlwind. She hardly felt the breeze that swirled around her legs.

She moved toward the door. "Then come on inside with me."

He followed and moved close to her while she unlocked the door, making her skin tingle. She hurriedly pushed it open and stepped inside. She dumped her purse and supply bag on the desk and went to the dangling lightbulb. She reached for the pull chain.

Gavin moved up behind her and slipped an arm around her waist. He exerted a gentle pressure while she held her breath and pulled. Light took the morning gloom from the room. Everything looked so bright. Having Gavin there with her made it all the more pleasant. She stepped back.

"This will mean a new kind of life for us here at school as well as elsewhere," she said, still staring at the bulb. "We'll be able to use the school and church buildings at night. Our pastor has already scheduled a service for Sunday evening."

Gavin nodded and moved so that he faced her. "Teachers will be able to do so many more things now."

She released a long, slow breath. "It's wonderful and exciting. I'm kind of sad that school will dismiss for the summer in only two weeks."

"You'll miss some things, but your sister will enjoy them."

Irene beamed. "That makes me happy."

His eyes locked on her face. Neither of them spoke for several moments. His expression told Irene she was not the only one remembering that kiss.

He cleared his throat. "Will you go on a picnic with me this weekend? We can take a lunch and hike along the creek."

She didn't have the willpower to turn him down. "When?".

"How about I pick you up at nine Saturday morning?"

"Can you make it a little later to give me time to get the laundry on the line?"

He nodded. "Is ten late enough?"

"Yes."

The sound of the door opening made them spring apart. Zada entered, and her eyes went to the dangling bulb. Her face broke into a glow that rivaled its radiance.

"Isn't it wonderful, Miss Delaney?"

Irene couldn't help but smile, at the girl as well as their shared joy. Zada had come out of a good deal of her shyness and become more open and outgoing lately.

After staring at the light a few more moments, Zada went on about her janitorial duties.

Gavin reached over, gave Irene's hand a squeeze and released it. "I'd better run or I'll be late for work. See you Saturday morning."

As he went out the door, two students entered.

Once class had assembled, Irene checked the roll and listened to them recite the Pledge of Allegiance to the flag. As soon as they finished and took their seats, Zada raised her hand.

"Yes, Zada."

"May we have a funeral for that?" She pointed at the lamp on the desk.

"Yeah, like they're doing in other places. I've heard Gavin talk about it." Wes didn't ask permission to speak as his enthusiasm bubbled forth.

"Please, Miss Delaney," came from another student.

When the whole class chimed in, Irene decided it would be all right. "How about Friday afternoon during the last hour of the school day?"

Heads bobbed, hands clapped, and students uttered expressions of approval.

"Since he's probably been to some of them, could Wes ask Gavin to read the obituary?" Zada asked cautiously.

"I'll ask him," Wes volunteered before Irene could answer.

"All right. We'll plan the service later. Right now we have lessons to study."

Chapter 14

Friday afternoon Gavin arrived shortly before the scheduled funeral, but he was not alone. Three men accompanied him.

Gavin smiled as they approached. "Irene, this is my boss, Joshua Maloney. These other two guys are Richard Wynn and Hadley Martin from our business office."

"Glad to meet you," she said, shaking the proffered hand of each man in turn.

"These mock funerals have set a humorous tone that's being repeated all across rural America," the one introduced as Joshua Maloney said.

Gavin spoke up. "Mr. Maloney has volunteered to deliver the sermon, but I'll do a short eulogy before it if you like."

"Of course." The sound of a motor drew Irene's attention to the road. A car pulled in, followed by a wagon. Soon a good-sized group of parents and community members had arrived and gathered near the electric pole in the back corner of the schoolyard. A paper-box coffin that held their kerosene lamp sat on a chair near the grave the older boys had dug at the base of the pole.

They conducted their service similar to ones they had heard about in other areas. Gavin delivered his eulogy, and then his boss delivered the funeral oration that was a mixture of tongue-in-cheek and serious words. Zada and Wesley served as pallbearers. The students sang "Let the Lower Lights Be Burning" as they lowered the casket into the hole.

When the song ended, the "mourners" cheered. Dirt was shoveled into the hole, and one of the co-op men placed a tombstone next to the spot. A sense of joy and accomplishment spilled from an emotional group.

Too involved to have spoken to Gavin personally, Irene watched as he and his colleagues walked away. When they reached the car his boss had driven, he looked over and waved at her, mouthing the words *See you tomorrow*.

When she got home, weary and drained, Irene had hardly set to work in the kitchen when an unfamiliar car pulled up outside. After a peek out the window, she put the curtain back in place and set the skillet down to go to the door.

A tall, distinguished man in a dark suit got out of the car and came to the porch steps. Someone from the co-op?

At the door, he removed his hat and extended a hand. "Hello, ma'am. Would you happen to be Miss Irene Delaney?"

"I would. How may I help you?"

He released her hand, his dark brown eyes doing a thorough inspection of her. "I'm Edwin Copley, a singing-school master, and I'm in need of a capable pianist. My wife usually travels with me and plays for my singing schools, but she broke her arm and can't play."

Irene's heart leaped as her mind raced ahead. He seemed legitimate, but she hesitated to invite a total stranger into the house with her dad not present. She indicated the porch swing.

"You're welcome to have a seat, Mr. Copley."

He shook his head. "Thank you, but I'm fine." He handed her an envelope. "Here's a letter of reference from the Hartford Music Institute. You're welcome to check my credentials. I'm a graduate of the institute and use their materials in my schools. I contacted them after Mona broke her arm and told them of my need. They gave me your name. I would like you to serve as my accompanist for this summer's series of schools if you will."

Oh, yes, the letter she had written the institute had contained her contact information, besides relating her qualifications. She tried to grasp what this stranger was saying. "You want me to travel with you and your wife this summer?"

"That's right. I can't pay you as much as you're worth, but I'll do the best I can for you." He named an amount. "I've talked to your pastor, who knows me, and he assured me of your talent and character."

A dozen thoughts ran through her in a dizzying tumult. After she'd checked the mail so closely every day, had a response to one of her letters just appeared in person? "Do you have to have an answer right now?"

"I realize you need some time to think and pray about it, and I assume you have family you need to consult. But our first school begins in two weeks. I need an answer within a couple of days."

That sounded fair enough under the circumstances. She inhaled a shallow breath. "Okay, I'll pray about it. How should I get in touch with you?"

"I'm staying with a friend in town. I'll come back Sunday afternoon."

"All right."

He placed his hat on his head, touched the brim of it and smiled. "Fine. I'll see you then."

Irene stood in silence as the man drove away. He seemed trustworthy, but she would go to town and use Rayona's telephone to call the school for a reference. Even as she completed the thought, it occurred to her that God had answered her prayer. He had provided a job for her, albeit another temporary one, but one that would be a ministry and might lead to bigger things.

Thank you, Lord. Please give me the wisdom and courage I need to know if this man is all he seems and whether I should go with him and his wife.

Her dad listened quietly during supper as Irene told him about her visitor and his request.

"Don't go unless you're absolutely sure it's what the Lord wants you to do," he said, his voice gruff. "You don't ever need to feel that you can't stay here with me."

Her heartstrings tugged so tight that tears blurred her vision. She made a hasty swipe at her eyes. "I know, Dad. But if God wants me to go, I have to be willing."

His eyes also took on a misty sheen. "I understand. Just be sure beyond a doubt."

That night Irene fell asleep praying.

"Thanks, Mom." Anticipation made Gavin's stomach quake as he accepted the picnic lunch she had prepared for him. He gave her a peck on the cheek. "Don't tell the kids where I've gone."

She smirked. "You mean Wesley. You're afraid he'll tease you."

He shrugged. "Guilty."

"Have fun. Now go before they come in from whatever they're doing." She nudged him toward the door.

When he got to the Delaney house and Irene came out to meet him, he watched the skirt of her green cotton dress swirl around her slim bare legs. Her midnight hair gleamed in the sunlight, beckoning him to move toward her faster. He laughed when they met on the porch steps and noted the basket at her feet. "We should have plenty to eat. I brought lunch."

She dimpled at him and didn't object when he picked up the basket. "So did I. But you look like a hungry boy."

He could only wonder at the power she had over him. She had turned his life upside down. He had decided that today he would tell her he loved her. He hoped desperately that she would say she loved him in return, that she would then belong exclusively to him. He wanted to know the kind of love that Riley Blake had with her sister.

"Is your laundry on the line?"

She gave him a quick smile. "All done."

He escorted her to his truck and placed her basket in the back next to his. "There's a place at the back of our farm that's perfect for a picnic. We call it Flat Rock because it's an area the size of a large house that's covered with a flat rock formation. It's where I've always sneaked off to when I wanted to be alone."

She looked over at him as he settled behind the wheel. "You can't be alone if you take me with you. Are you sure you want to share your private place with me?"

"Yes, and I'm being sneaky to do it. I'm going to drive around the back way to the farm and park far enough away that the kids, Wes in particular, don't know we're there."

A trill of laughter came from her lips. "You're devious. And I'm devious enough to appreciate it. I want to spend at least part of a day free from the responsibilities of work. I want to play."

She looked and sounded so young and full of life. Her joy was contagious. If he had harbored any lingering doubts that he loved her, they were now gone. He backed the truck up and sped down the road. The spring foliage each side of the road added to his sense of joy and well-being.

Five minutes later he pulled off onto a side road that was little more than a two-rutted path with a strip of grass growing down the middle. A hundred yards or so into it he pulled over and parked next to a big oak tree. He hopped out and came around the truck to meet Irene.

Sudden warmth filled him as she slipped from the seat and stood next to him. Their faces only inches apart, he could hardly breathe. Every nerve in his body hummed like the power in those lines he saw and worked with every day.

He released her hand to get the baskets.

"Let me carry one." She stretched out a hand.

Seizing an opportunity, he handed her one, being careful to put it in her left hand. Then he reclaimed her right one with his left. Her hand in his felt right as he led her to the picnic spot.

"It's beautiful, so scenic and restful." She gazed around at the rock-furnished glade, her awe-filled voice sending a shiver through him. She inhaled deeply. "The air smells so clean and sweet."

As much as he hated to, he released her hand. "Let's put our food on that big rock and go for a walk before we eat."

She set her basket down, and he put his beside it. "There are trails all around here. Do you have a preference which way we go?"

She looked around in contemplation and then pointed to the east. "Let's try that one."

They set off in that direction. Gavin wanted to take her hand again but decided he shouldn't be pushy. He was entranced when a spring breeze lifted strands of her hair across her face and she brushed it back behind her ears. He wanted to touch it so badly but resisted.

"This is perfect," she said as she came to a halt on their way down a bare slope. "We can have salad before lunch."

He watched in amusement as she plucked the leaves from a sheep sorrel plant. He grinned and accepted her offering when she handed him half the fistful she had gathered. He would probably have accepted it even if he didn't like the stuff.

"I love the tart taste of this," she said, putting a leaf into her mouth.

He nodded. "Me too. The flavor reminds me of rhubarb or gooseberries." He stuffed a couple of leaves in his mouth and chewed.

"Jolene and I would roam the field when I was a kid. She taught me to find and eat it."

Still munching, they resumed walking. As they finished their woodland salad they worked their way in a circle back to the picnic spot and arrived just in time to spot a raccoon snooping into one of the baskets.

Gavin dashed ahead of Irene. "Shoo. Get out of there," he called, waving his hands to scare it away. When it was gone, he checked under the tablecloth his mother had put on top of the food.

"We were just in time," he said as Irene reached her basket. "I guess we should eat before the wild creatures get it."

They spread the tablecloth over a flat area and sat on each side of it to lay out the food. They ate his mother's fried chicken and cheese, along with Irene's apples and homemade bread, and drank the bottles of soda he had brought. Gavin wished he could stop time. The day was so perfect he didn't want it to end.

When they finished eating, Irene tucked the leftovers and supplies back into the baskets. His heartbeat thundered in his ears as he watched her, trying to gauge the right moment to bare his heart to her.

When she left the baskets and returned to her seat on the rocks, he edged closer. She looked over at him, her lips curved slightly at the corners.

Didn't she know the effect she had on him? She was heart-stoppingly beautiful, strong and talented—the woman with whom he wanted to share the rest of his life.

Their gazes held as something intense and nerve shattering passed between them. He exerted fierce mental control to keep from making a fool of himself. He had to say this right.

Suddenly her smile widened. "I had a visitor after I got home yesterday."

He struggled to speak through his dry mouth, diverted from what he had been preparing to say. "Someone interesting?"

She nodded, her eyes sparkling with life. "He introduced himself as Edwin Copley, a singing-school master connected to the Hartford Music Institute. He asked me to travel with him and his wife this summer and accompany the singing and vocal exercises at his schools. His wife normally plays, but she broke her arm and won't be able to play for a long time."

His heart trembled as the import of her words began to sink in. She would leave once school ended. A hollowness formed in his middle as he listened to her describe the man and tell how she had gone to town early this morning and called the president of the music school and gotten a glowing reference regarding the man's qualifications and character.

She had so much talent, so much heart, to offer. He could not ask her to give up her calling and stay here to marry him. He loved her too much to stand in her way.

He had to enjoy the moment and store up memories for the future.

Irene began to pray as soon as Gavin delivered her home and drove away.

Lord, please teach me as You promised. Guide me along the path You have for me.

Weird, disjointed dreams woke her several times through the night. The used washing machine she had planned to buy from Rayona's parents laughed at her. Dad laughed when she had to sleep on top of the piano at singing schools. Jolene and Riley laughed when she had to ride on the roof of Mr. Copley's car. But Gavin did not laugh. His tender looks and quiet acceptance of her departure made her wake with tears wetting her face.

Yet deep in her heart, she had the answer for which she had prayed. She had to go. She shared the news with her dad over breakfast.

He stared across the table at her, his face solemn. "Do what you must. You know the way home if anything changes."

She nodded and dabbed at her lips with a napkin. "I'll finish the commitment, no matter what, because I believe it's what God would have me do."

After church they went home with Jolene and Riley for dinner. As she and Jolene washed dishes afterward, Irene related the invitation from Mr. Copley and the decision she had reached.

"You know we'll support you." Jolene spoke brightly, but her mouth quivered slightly. "I'll keep an eye on Dad, see that he eats and do his laundry with ours." She wiped her hands on her apron and hugged Irene. "When do you leave?"

Irene swallowed and backed away. "I'll find out the exact date when I give Mr. Copley my answer this afternoon. And I need to get home so I'll be there when he comes."

"Go on. I'll finish in here." Jolene shooed her out of the kitchen. "Follow your dreams." She turned her back quickly, and Irene saw her make a furtive swipe at her eyes.

That afternoon part of her was glad when Mr. Copley asked if she could be ready the following Sunday afternoon, a week earlier than his first school started. He wanted her to spend that week with him and his wife so they could work together and go over everything he planned to do in the singing schools and the materials he planned to use.

The week passed in a whirl. Irene stayed too busy to think about anything but the final days of school, letting her piano students know she was leaving and getting packed. She didn't see Gavin all week.

As he waited outside the church after services Sunday, Gavin's stomach lurched and rolled. He couldn't bear to say goodbye to Irene, but he couldn't let her go without doing it. When she emerged, he stepped to her side.

He started to speak and couldn't get the words through his tight throat. He tried again. "I understand you're leaving this afternoon. I wish you the best."

He wanted to hold her, keep her here with him for the rest of their lives. But he wanted her to be happy.

She flashed him a smile. "Thank you. All I want is to be wherever God wants me, doing His will."

"I know you're using your talent how you feel He wants of you. I admire you for that." *But, oh, how I'll miss you.* "I guess I won't see you again for a long time."

She nodded. "Mr. Copley said the last school he has scheduled for this summer ends just before Labor Day."

He felt guilty for detaining her when others were waiting to speak to her. He gave her a lopsided smile that didn't quite work. The muscles in his neck twitched, knotted until he could hardly breathe. "Think of me sometime?"

She nodded, her look solemn. "Count on it."

He fought for control. "Take care."

He watched her make her way through other well-wishers and get in the car with her dad. He sighed and turned to join his own family. But a hand on his shoulder made him turn. To his surprise, it was Pastor Jacob.

"Gavin, do you have a moment?"

"Of course." He followed the man to the edge of the yard, where they could speak in private.

"I've been talking to your mother. She told me what a difference there has been in Wesley's behavior since you returned home. She gives you credit for it."

"I haven't done much, just spent some time with him."

The pastor's head nodded in approval. "Exactly what he needed. We have other boys in the church who could benefit from some quality male companionship. Would you consider helping us organize some activities for the boys in that general age group?"

Gavin frowned. "What kind of activities?"

The pastor grinned. "That's what I'm hoping you'll figure out. You found things to do with Wesley. Surely you can think of things a group could do together."

"You mean something as simple as baseball?"

He shrugged. "If that's what you want to do, it's fine with me. It would be wonderful if you could have recreation with them but also get them involved in some kind of missionary projects."

"Nothing of that sort comes to mind."

"You'll think of something. The Bible says in the third chapter of Proverbs, 'Trust in the Lord with all thine heart, and lean not unto thine own understanding. In all thy ways acknowledge Him, and He shall direct thy paths.'" The man turned and left.

Gavin pondered what had just been asked of him. He knew nothing about working with the church, or teenage boys, but the verse came back to him. *Trust in the Lord.*

He inhaled deeply and resumed his way to the truck. *Okay, God, but I'll have to have Your help, a lot of it.*

Chapter 15

A crater formed in Irene's heart as Mr. Copley's car carried them south that evening. She had wanted to reach out and stroke Gavin's rigid jawline, to feel his arms around her. But she had managed to restrain herself. The salty taste of tears nearly strangled her as she fought to keep her composure and not disturb the couple in the front seat. She was thankful to be sitting in the back, with darkness hiding her face.

Her stomach rolled. Afraid of being carsick, she leaned back in the seat and tried to keep from retching.

Since she had learned to drive, there'd been no occasion for her to have to ride in the backseat of anyone's car. She had forgotten how sick she used to get when riding in the back, figuring she had outgrown it. She hadn't. But she couldn't ask Mrs. Copley to exchange seats with her. No way.

By the time they reached the Copley's house, Irene

was miserable. Barely able to function, she fought to stay on her feet and spoke only when addressed. Thankfully, she was shown directly to the room she would occupy that week. As soon as she was alone, she crawled into bed, so sick she feared she could never get up.

Over the following weeks, a pattern formed as they began to travel. Through trial and error Irene learned some strategies that helped her survive the nausea, cold sweats and dizziness when on the road. When salty crackers, fresh water and other tricks didn't work, she simply closed her eyes and slept if she could.

She wasn't sorry she had left Deer Lick, but sharp pangs of nostalgia struck her when memories of Gavin got a grip on her.

Why had she let him slip out of her life?

She had to constantly remind herself it was because she wanted to use her talent for God.

Over the summer they settled into a routine. Irene loved the thrill of playing for the classes and singing along with the beloved hymns and gospel songs. Adrenaline flooded her veins when the people clapped and sang. But even though she was surrounded by people most of the time, she found that she could still feel lonesome in the crowds. She missed Gavin. She missed her dad and Jolene. Her life in Deer Lick seemed dim and far away.

They spent long hours in churches, meeting a constant stream of new people and strange faces. Irene lived out of her suitcase in the homes of host families she had to get to know and then leave behind. By the end of summer, Irene was ready to go home. When Mr. Copley got behind the wheel for the final trip, she crawled into her spot in the rear and lolled her head back against the seat.

Although the time had seemed to drag, now it felt that the weeks had gone by in a whirl.

"Are you anxious to get home?" Mrs. Copley asked over her shoulder.

Irene had to be truthful. "I can't wait to see my dad and sister." *And Gavin.*

"Is there a young man waiting for you?" The plump woman twisted around in the seat so she could see Irene.

"There's someone who's important to me, but I don't know that he's waiting for me."

The woman chuckled. "Oh, I'm sure he is."

"What is your opinion of the summer?" Mr. Copley interjected.

Irene peered forward into the darkening sky. "I enjoyed it, and I learned a lot. Everyone treated us like royalty." *But this is not the life for me.*

"I'll give you a good reference at the music institute. I understood that you're interested in working for them."

"I was," she admitted frankly. "But I'm not sure what's in my future now."

What she did know was that living on the road was impossible for her. Whatever ministry she had would be in Deer Lick.

"God will show you."

"I know."

Gavin's heart leaped when he heard that Irene had returned home. He wanted to run straight to her house and welcome her, hold her in his arms. But he didn't want to betray his feelings and scare her away.

He had drowned himself in work all summer, working all day at his job, doing chores at home in the evenings and spending weekends with the boys of the church. They had become a group by forming a baseball team. When they heard that Mr. Harris had fallen and cracked a rib, they had taken turns going there daily to check on the man and do whatever he needed done. They continued until Mr. Harris had healed enough to resume his normal routine.

Other needs had been brought to their attention, and they had met each challenge, helping people around the countryside. Through the experiences, Gavin had come to know the joy of having an impact on the boys and the satisfaction in having the Lord use him. The power of God had become real to him.

"Hey, what are you doing there?"

Wes's shout snapped Gavin out of his wool gathering. He put down the ax he had been holding, staring at it mindlessly.

"You aimin' to come after me with that?" Wes teased.

Gavin shook his head, as if to clear it of cobwebs. "Not today."

Wes glanced around. "You don't seem like you're too anxious to cut wood. I got my pile finished, so I think I'll go to the school."

That seemed odd. Wes would be starting high school in town next week. Had he decided he would miss the rural school? "The school?"

"Yeah. I rode the doodlebug over there yesterday, and I lost my knife. Do you have time to help me look for it?"

Gavin considered. He wasn't in the mood to cut wood, but he wanted to be sure Mom had enough for the kitchen stove. "I'll go as soon as I finish this." He nodded at the small pile left to split.

Wes's face broke into a grin. "I'll take the doodlebug and beat you there." He hopped onto it and roared off.

Gavin finished the wood and carried it inside. Then he headed for the school.

* * *

Irene took a leisurely bath and washed her hair. Then she put on a comfortable pink-print dress and went out on the porch. The afternoon sun shone brightly, and a gentle breeze rustled through the trees.

She was sitting in the porch swing brushing her hair when she spied Zada Lonigan walking up the road. When she got near the house, Zada turned into the yard and came up to the porch.

"Hi, Miss Delaney. I'm glad you're back."

Irene smiled. "It's good to be home. How did you spend your summer?"

The girl wrinkled her nose. "Oh, the usual. I worked in the garden, picked berries and helped Mama can stuff for winter. And I spent time with Wes," she added with a shy grin.

Irene's smile broadened. "You two have become close friends, haven't you?"

"Yes, ma'am." Zada smiled self-consciously. "Gavin started a baseball team for the boys of the church this summer. And they did a lot of work for people who were sick or hurt. The pastor calls them when he needs anything."

Irene's heart swelled at hearing of Gavin's involvement in the church and of his work with the boys. She swallowed against the lump that rose in her throat.

The girl's expression turned serious. "Yesterday Wes took me for a ride on their doodlebug. While we were riding around the schoolyard, we noticed that somebody has been digging around our grave."

Irene frowned. "You mean where we buried the lamp?"

Zada's head bobbed. "I'm gonna stop by the school and check on it again. Will you go with me?"

Irene couldn't imagine why anyone would bother their

grave site. She wouldn't be returning to the school as teacher, but she felt responsible for the place. She dragged the brush through her tresses. "As soon as I get my hair dry, I'll drive us there."

The girl brightened. "Oh, good. But you don't need to take me. I'll cut across the woods and field and beat you there," she called as she turned and took off at a run.

Irene watched her crawl through the barbed-wire fence on the other side of the road and sprint into the woods. Bemused, she finished drying her hair and went to get the car keys.

When she drove into the schoolyard, Irene saw Gavin's truck parked near the building. He stood next to it, leaning back against the driver's-side door. The sight of his tanned forearms below the rolled-up sleeves of his blue cotton shirt made her gulp for air.

She blinked, her heart leaping like a deer. Her eyes darted side to side, looking for Zada. There was no sign of her. Irene parked next to the truck and took a calming breath before she got out.

"Welcome back," Gavin greeted her as he pushed himself away from his truck.

"Thank you." The emotions crashing through her made the words come out in a breathless rush.

His warm gaze rested on her face, searching as it moved over her mouth, chin and eyes. "Will you be staying awhile, or are you leaving again?"

She smiled, her mouth gone dry. "I'm home for good."

He frowned. "You mean the trip was a mistake?"

She shook her head. "Oh, no, it was a good thing. God had a lesson for me to learn."

He waited.

How could she explain what it had taken her all summer to learn? "For some reason we seem to think that answering God's call means going where everything is bigger, where there are more people. I had to go to some bigger places to understand that size means nothing. Substance is everything. People in small places also need to be taught, sung to and evangelized. The key is *how* we serve, not where. If we serve with all our hearts, our little place in the world is not a stepping-stone to success. It *is* success."

His face took on an odd look. "Do you mean Deer Lick?"

She nodded.

He hesitated. "You're really back for good?"

"This is my home. Whatever ministry I have is right here." She glanced around, suddenly remembering why she had come. "What are you doing here?"

"Wes said he lost his knife and asked me to come help him find it. He got on the doodlebug and left ahead of me. But he's not here. Why are you here?"

A niggle of suspicion crept up her spine. "Zada asked me to meet her here and took off ahead of me. But she's not here either."

His mouth formed a funny twist. "What excuse did she give?"

"She said she thinks someone has been digging around our grave site and asked if I would come with her to check on it."

He turned to stare over at the site. "I smell a plot. Shall we look for clues?"

Trying to control the wild beating of her heart, yet curious, Irene nodded. "We may as well." The words came out airy and barely audible.

He reached for her hand and drew her along with him. At the grave site they stood and stared at the little mound of dirt and the tombstone. "No sign of digging," he said.

"And no knife," she added. Then she spotted two pieces of folded paper at the base of the electric pole, each anchored with a rock.

As one, they stepped toward them. Gavin leaned down and picked up one. He glanced at it. "This one has your name on it." He handed it to her and reached for the other one. "This one is addressed to me."

Irene unfolded the paper and read.

Dear Miss Delaney,
You love Wesley's brother. Do something about it.
Zada

She looked up, too numb to speak. Gavin raised his head, an expression on his face that had to match the one on hers.

"You can read mine if I can read yours," he said in a strained voice. He held it out.

Trembling, Irene reached for it with one hand while passing her note to him with the other. With a sense of impending disaster she read the second note.

Dear Gavin,
You love Miss Delaney. You better ask her to marry you before I do.
Wes

When she looked up this time, Gavin had a hand over his mouth, whether to cover laughter or an apology…or she didn't know what.

"Do you think he means he'll ask me to marry *him* or…you." She nearly strangled on the question.

Gavin removed his hand from his mouth. "I hope he means he'll ask you to marry me. Are they right?"

Irene could not deny that the kids were right, but she was afraid to admit it.

He looked up at the top of the pole. "Wes is right about me. He knows you're the light of my life. I love you, Irene."

She stood stone still as he moved nearer and cupped the side of her face with his hand. He tipped it up and peered directly into her eyes, searching.

Irene's knees went so weak that she sagged against him. When he wrapped his arms around her, she raised hers and slipped them around his neck. "I love you, Gavin."

His embrace tightened, and his head dipped. When his lips met hers in a deep yet gentle kiss, she went up on tiptoe and returned it with a heart full of joy.

When Gavin lifted his head, she couldn't bring herself to release him. She stared up into his face. "I love you," she repeated, glorying in letting the words she had guarded in her heart for so long come spilling out. A mist formed in her eyes.

His mouth spread into a beaming smile. "Does that mean you'll marry me if Wesley asks you?"

She smirked. "I prefer you do the asking."

All teasing left his expression. "I love you, Irene. I'm not rich, but I've saved part of my wages during the years I've been with the company. I can support a family. Will you marry me and have that family with me?"

She blinked back tears and placed a hand on his cheek. "Gavin, I wouldn't care if you had nothing. I'll marry you because I love you and don't want to live my life without you."

He pulled her to him and claimed her lips in a forever kind of kiss. Then he spun her gently around before lowering her back to solid footing.

Irene smiled up at him and then gazed on up at the electric lines above them. And marveled at such power. But it dimmed in comparison to the power of God—and love.

Epilogue

Jolene smoothed the folds of Irene's wedding dress into place, looking after her as she had always done. She adjusted the veil and stepped back, her eyes shiny with tears. Then she took Irene's hands in her own and squeezed them.

"You are such a beautiful bride. And I'm so happy for you. But I don't know whether to laugh or cry." She did a little of both.

Irene smiled at her sister and swallowed the lump in her throat, her own eyes welling. "You've always been there for me."

"Now Gavin will be there for you." Jolene smiled through her tears. "It's time for you to have this."

Irene watched, transfixed, as Jolene reached behind her neck, unclasped the locket she wore and held it out.

Irene knew how much Jolene treasured that locket. She kept it locked in her jewelry box and only took it out for special occasions. It had belonged to their mother, and it contained a picture of their small family when Jolene was about twelve and Irene just a toddler.

"I can't take that," she said, drawing back.

Jolene pressed it into her hand. "I've had it the ten years since Mom died. You should have it now."

Reluctant to take it but unable to refuse, Irene allowed her sister to place it around her neck. "All right, but ten years from now you get it back."

"Fine, we'll take turns. Now you're ready." Jolene stepped back to gaze at her in approval. "Oh, no, you need these." She took the bouquet of white gardenias and red roses from the table and placed it in Irene's arms.

The sound of piano music signaled that it was time. Together they left the classroom they had used as a dressing room and went to the hallway, where Sam, Callie and Callie's daughter Lily waited in front of the closed door. Sam opened it and Lily led the way, strewing flowers from a small basket.

Jolene gave Irene a last quick hug and followed the little girl.

Sam stepped up beside Irene and crooked his arm. "It's hard to give you away," he said, his voice cracking. "But Gavin is a good man."

Clutching her bouquet in one hand, Irene placed her other hand on her dad's arm and moved to the open doorway with him. When the music changed to the "Wedding March," they moved down the aisle. Irene aimed a smile at the pianist, her most advanced student, and surveyed the two pews near the piano where the rest of her students sat.

Vases of colorful mums and other bright fall flowers graced the sills of windows through which clear sunshine illuminated the family and friends gathered to witness their simple wedding.

Irene looked forward and saw Gavin, so handsome

in his black suit, standing next to Wes and watching her approach, his eyes gleaming with adoration.

The ceremony passed in a blur. A different student accompanied her uncle's quartet in a song. Then they repeated their vows and exchanged rings. Before it seemed possible, they were at their reception in the big room at the back of the little church.

Against one wall was a piano, where Irene's students went to the instrument one by one, played two pieces of contrasting styles and left so the next student could perform. Contentment, and just a little pride, flowed through her as they provided background music for the reception.

Within days of her return home she had resumed lessons with her piano students and quickly added more, including a couple of adults who wanted to learn to play. Students who could pay for lessons did. If they could not, she taught them anyhow. She had made arrangements with Zada and the two oldest Holman girls similar to the one Pearl Harris had made with her years earlier. Each did a weekly chore in exchange for lessons.

Irene knew in her heart that she was where she should be, doing what the Lord would have her do. Churches and singing groups in the area would have accompanists for years to come.

Jolene and Callie served the wedding cake, iced tea, lemonade and coffee. As soon as everyone had been served, Irene and Gavin joined their blended family at a table. Riley Blake held his and Jolene's small son, while Trace Gentry corralled his and Callie's twins and infant daughter. Lily sat with her friends at another table. Gavin's mother and Irene and Jolene's dad sat at the end of the table. They had become such good friends that Juanita had given up on Sam.

"Have you made a decision yet?" Irene asked her sister.

Jolene put her tea down. "I'm still sad, but we've decided I should try it for a year."

"If she's not happy teaching in town, she can quit and stay home, maybe have another baby." Her husband's mouth spread in a happy grin as he let the wiggling child in his lap slide to the floor. "Oops, I'd better catch him before he yanks something off the table." He started after little Rolen as the child toddled toward the refreshment table.

Jolene had recently been informed that the Deer Creek School had been consolidated into the town school, and it would close at the end of that school year. The school board had assured her she would have a position in the town school if she wanted it, even if they had to create a job for her.

Irene nodded. "That sounds like a good plan."

"How soon do you two think you can start work on your house?" Trace asked as he placed little Linda on the floor to pursue her brothers.

"Probably not before spring," Gavin answered.

As Jolene and Riley had done, Irene and Gavin would live with Sam while building a house on the acreage Irene had been given as a wedding gift.

Gavin took Irene's hand and leaned over to whisper in her ear. "I think we can escape now."

Irene glanced around at the women wiping tables and clearing debris. "Let's go."

They slipped out the door and hurried down the hall to the front door. Once on the front porch, they paused to inhale the crisp fall air, and then they embraced. Her heart swelling to bursting, Irene thanked God for Gavin and his growing commitment to God. For her family. For love.

Gavin drew back but kept an arm around her as he gazed down into her face. "This is home. This church.

This town. The house we'll build here. We belong here—
together. I'll do my best to keep you happy."

Irene's eyes met his, unmindful of the sound of rushing feet approaching from behind. "You're right. And
this was the perfect wedding, because you're the perfect
man for me."

"And you're perfect for me," he said, drawing her to
him for a kiss that promised a lifetime of happiness.

* * * * *

REQUEST YOUR FREE BOOKS!

2 FREE INSPIRATIONAL NOVELS
PLUS 2
FREE
MYSTERY GIFTS

Love Inspired™

YES! Please send me 2 FREE Love Inspired® novels and my 2 FREE mystery gifts (gifts are worth about $10). After receiving them, if I don't wish to receive any more books, I can return the shipping statement marked "cancel." If I don't cancel, I will receive 6 brand-new novels every month and be billed just $4.74 per book in the U.S. or $5.24 per book in Canada. That's a savings of at least 21% off the cover price. It's quite a bargain! Shipping and handling is just 50¢ per book in the U.S. and 75¢ per book in Canada.* I understand that accepting the 2 free books and gifts places me under no obligation to buy anything. I can always return a shipment and cancel at any time. Even if I never buy another book, the two free books and gifts are mine to keep forever.

105/305 IDN F49N

Name _____ (PLEASE PRINT) _____

Address _____ Apt. # _____

City _____ State/Prov. _____ Zip/Postal Code _____

Signature (if under 18, a parent or guardian must sign)

Mail to the Harlequin® Reader Service:
IN U.S.A.: P.O. Box 1867, Buffalo, NY 14240-1867
IN CANADA: P.O. Box 609, Fort Erie, Ontario L2A 5X3

**Are you a subscriber to Love Inspired books
and want to receive the larger-print edition?**
Call 1-800-873-8635 or visit www.ReaderService.com.

* Terms and prices subject to change without notice. Prices do not include applicable taxes. Sales tax applicable in N.Y. Canadian residents will be charged applicable taxes. Offer not valid in Quebec. This offer is limited to one order per household. Not valid for current subscribers to Love Inspired books. All orders subject to credit approval. Credit or debit balances in a customer's account(s) may be offset by any other outstanding balance owed by or to the customer. Please allow 4 to 6 weeks for delivery. Offer available while quantities last.

Your Privacy—The Harlequin® Reader Service is committed to protecting your privacy. Our Privacy Policy is available online at www.ReaderService.com or upon request from the Harlequin Reader Service.
We make a portion of our mailing list available to reputable third parties that offer products we believe may interest you. If you prefer that we not exchange your name with third parties, or if you wish to clarify or modify your communication preferences, please visit us at www.ReaderService.com/consumerchoice or write to us at Harlequin Reader Service Preference Service, P.O. Box 9062, Buffalo, NY 14269. Include your complete name and address.

LIDIR13R

REQUEST YOUR FREE BOOKS!

2 FREE INSPIRATIONAL NOVELS
PLUS 2
FREE
MYSTERY GIFTS

Love Inspired
HISTORICAL
INSPIRATIONAL HISTORICAL ROMANCE

YES! Please send me 2 FREE Love Inspired® Historical novels and my 2 FREE
mystery gifts (gifts are worth about $10). After receiving them, if I don't wish to receive
any more books, I can return the shipping statement marked "cancel." If I don't cancel,
I will receive 4 brand-new novels every month and be billed just $4.74 per book in the
U.S. or $5.24 per book in Canada. That's a savings of at least 21% off the cover price.
It's quite a bargain! Shipping and handling is just 50¢ per book in the U.S. and 75¢ per
book in Canada.* I understand that accepting the 2 free books and gifts places me under
no obligation to buy anything. I can always return a shipment and cancel at any time.
Even if I never buy another book, the two free books and gifts are mine to keep forever.

102/302 IDN F5CY

Name _____
(PLEASE PRINT)

Address _____ Apt. #

City _____ State/Prov. _____ Zip/Postal Code

Signature (if under 18, a parent or guardian must sign)

Mail to the **Harlequin® Reader Service:**
IN U.S.A.: P.O. Box 1867, Buffalo, NY 14240-1867
IN CANADA: P.O. Box 609, Fort Erie, Ontario L2A 5X3

Want to try two free books from another series?
Call 1-800-873-8635 or visit www.ReaderService.com.

* Terms and prices subject to change without notice. Prices do not include applicable
taxes. Sales tax applicable in N.Y. Canadian residents will be charged applicable taxes.
Offer not valid in Quebec. This offer is limited to one order per household. Not valid
for current subscribers to Love Inspired Historical books. All orders subject to credit
approval. Credit or debit balances in a customer's account(s) may be offset by any other
outstanding balance owed by or to the customer. Please allow 4 to 6 weeks for delivery.
Offer available while quantities last.

Your Privacy—The Harlequin® Reader Service is committed to protecting your
privacy. Our Privacy Policy is available online at www.ReaderService.com or upon
request from the Harlequin Reader Service.

We make a portion of our mailing list available to reputable third parties that offer
products we believe may interest you. If you prefer that we not exchange your name with
third parties, or if you wish to clarify or modify your communication preferences, please
visit us at www.ReaderService.com/consumerchoice or write to us at Harlequin Reader
Service Preference Service, P.O. Box 9062, Buffalo, NY 14269. Include your complete
name and address.

LIHDIR13R

ReaderService.com

Manage your account online!

- Review your order history
- Manage your payments
- Update your address

*We've designed
the Harlequin® Reader Service
website just for you.*

Enjoy all the features!

- Reader excerpts from any series
- Respond to mailings and
  special monthly offers
- Discover new series available to you
- Browse the Bonus Bucks catalog
- Share your feedback

Visit us at:

ReaderService.com

RS13